YARD
WAR

TAYLOR KITCHINGS

YARD WAR

WENDY
LAMB
BOOKS

Text copyright © 2015 by Taylor Kitchings
Jacket art copyright © 2015 by Jeff Wack

All rights reserved. Published in the United States by Wendy Lamb Books, an imprint of Random House Children's Books, a division of Penguin Random House LLC, New York.

Wendy Lamb Books and the colophon are trademarks of Penguin Random House LLC.

Visit us on the Web! randomhousekids.com

Educators and librarians, for a variety of teaching tools, visit us at RHTeachersLibrarians.com

Library of Congress Cataloging-in-Publication Data
Kitchings, Taylor, author.
The all-out yard war / Taylor Kitchings. — First edition.
pages cm
ISBN 978-0-553-50753-9 (trade) — ISBN 978-0-553-50754-6 (lib. bdg.) —
ISBN 978-0-553-50756-0 (pbk.) — ISBN 978-0-553-50755-3 (ebook)
1. Racism—Juvenile fiction. 2. Race relations—Juvenile fiction. 3. African
Americans—Juvenile fiction. 4. Football stories. 5. Neighbors—Juvenile fiction.
6. Families—Mississippi—Juvenile fiction. 7. Nineteen sixties—Juvenile fiction.
8. Jackson (Miss.)—History—Juvenile fiction. [1. Racism—Fiction. 2. Race
relations—Fiction. 3. African Americans—Fiction. 4. Football—Fiction.
5. Neighbors—Fiction. 6. Family life—Mississippi—Fiction. 7. Nineteen
sixties—Fiction. 8. Jackson (Miss.)—History—20th century—Fiction.] I. Title.
PZ7.1.K63A1 2015
[Fic]—dc23
2014040326

The text of this book is set in 12.5-point Berling.
Jacket design by Sarah Hokanson
Interior design by Trish Parcell

Printed in the United States of America
10 9 8 7 6 5 4 3 2 1
First Edition

For Beth, my love, light, and patient muse

Whoever invented football was thinking about a day like today. Fall in Mississippi is always hot to cool, cool to hot, like it can't make up its mind whether it's really fall until it's too late and time for Christmas— but today the air was that perfect in-between that makes you run twice as fast. There weren't any clouds and the sky was extra high and the blue was extra blue, like God had been holding back all summer.

The guys were coming over after lunch to get up a game, and it was hard to wait that long. I went out to the front yard to practice my routes.

Hut one! Hut two! Hut three!

I take off down the yard, runnin' *hard*, all the way to the rose bed, and when I look around, the ball is almost there, and the defender jumps up and gets a hand on it, but I jump even higher and yank it away from him and dive into the end zone, and the announcer screams *"Woo-hoo, mercy!"* and the crowd goes wild—and I didn't hurt a single one of Mama's roses.

I'd make that catch for the Donelson Dirt Daubers if Mama and Daddy would let me go out for football. They say seventh grade is a "difficult transition," and I have to wait till I get a little bigger and my grades get a little better—well, a *lot* better. "What about the fact that I was co-first-string split end at McWinkle last year?" I say. "Junior high is a whole different deal," they say.

I get down at the edge of the rose bed and take off the other way, even faster, with two safeties and a cornerback right on my tail, and the Rebels are losing with only five seconds left in the game, and the quarterback lets it fly fifty yards into triple coverage, and I jump higher than any split end has ever jumped in the history of football, I mean up there with the *trees*, and I snag the ball with one hand and crash into the end zone, and the announcer screams, *"Woo-hoo . . ."*

"Dadgummit!"

It's okay to say "dadgummit"—Daddy says it—especially if you slide on the driveway and rip the scab off your knee, plus rip the jeans your mama just bought after you ripped your other jeans. I'm not afraid of blood, but I went inside to get Willie Jane to put mercurochrome on it and see if she'd do some sewing right quick while Mama was still at the country club.

Willie Jane was ironing and watching Ginny Lynn so she wouldn't eat her Play-Doh, which she will do, I've seen her.

"Can't fix it," she said, barely looking up from her ironing.

"Please, Willie Jane."

"Unh-unh, it's not torn at the seam. Can't make it look right."

"You can try."

"Child, I got work to do. What you doin' out there sliding around in your new jeans anyway? Nobody can play football by himself."

"Well, Farish is down at the Gibsons', and you're ironin', and Ginny Lynn is four, so who am I supposed to play with?"

"You could ask Dee. He's been workin' all morning without taking a break. He could use one."

I looked in the backyard, and there was Dee in an old red shirt, stretching as far as he could with the rake, pulling it in hard. He's pretty skinny and short to be almost eleven, but I never saw anybody get a yard so clean. I'm almost twelve and a half, and I could handle the mowing and raking myself, but Mama said she wanted Dee to do it because he and Willie Jane need the money.

Okay, I thought, why not? I'll ask Dee if he wants to pass it around a little. I stuffed the torn jeans in the closet and changed into some old ones. It should have been a simple thing to go out there and ask him. But when I started to pull on the sliding glass door, something stopped me. It took a second to know what it was: I almost never talked to colored people. I *heard* a lot about colored people, especially lately, but except for Willie Jane, or Meemaw's maid or a waiter at the club or the guy at the Texaco, I didn't talk to any. I had definitely never asked a colored kid to throw a football with me. I mean, I said hi to him, and he was Willie Jane's son, after all, but still. . . .

Willie Jane came into the kitchen and saw me looking outside, spinning the ball and not going anywhere.

"You gonna ask him?" she said.

There wasn't any way to explain why I wouldn't, so I went on out there.

"Tell Dee it's just a short break," she said. "I'll make some pimiento cheese for y'all's lunch in a little while and then he can get back to work."

I walked down the yard, spinning the ball high as I could get it, catching it as I went.

"Hey, Dee."

He looked up from his rake and wiped his forehead.

"Hey, Trip."

"Your mom said you can take a break. Wanna throw the ball with me?"

"Oh, I better not do that." He looked up at the house like he needed permission just to be talking to me.

"Come on. She said it was okay, I promise."

He wiped his forehead some more and looked around. "Well . . . maybe just for a minute. Can we do it back here?"

The backyard is no good for football. It's straight downhill and full of oak trees all the way to the creek. Plus, Mama has a couple of flower beds running across it to trip you. Plus, the creek would have to be the goal line and every time you scored a touchdown you'd drown. But I said okay.

I couldn't tell if Dee really wanted to throw with me or just thought he was supposed to. He was acting pretty shy. If I never got much chance to talk to colored people, maybe he had even less chance to talk to white people.

Willie Jane stuck her head out the door and yelled for us to watch the flowers, 'cause Mama had just planted a bunch of daffodils to keep the moles away.

I tossed the ball to Dee.

"You sure do a good job," I told him. "I never saw a yardman so careful."

He smiled. "My mama say if you don't do it right the first time, you must have time to do it over."

We started out fairly close together, just passing it back and forth. He was throwing nothing but spirals and putting it right in my hands. Gradually, we backed up from each other, the way guys do, to see which one will say "That's far enough." Pretty soon he was way over on one side of the yard, and I was way over on the other, and neither one of us had said it.

I heaved it hard as I could, and the ball landed ten feet in front of him. But Dee drew back and hit me in the hands, *zip*, easy as pie. I suddenly got the terrible feeling that this skinny little colored kid could throw a football better than me. Then I thought, Well, that's okay, I'm not a quarterback, I'm a split end—I'm sure he can't hang on to a pass like I can. And he can't run nearly as fast.

We got to talkin' a little. I listened harder than usual.

"So you play a lot of ball?" I asked him.

"I throw a Wiffle ball at school."

"What are y'all?"

"I don't know. A bunch of kids on a playground."

"I mean, what's the name of y'all's team at school?"

"Ain't got a team," he said. "I might have a team when I go to junior high next year."

"Well, you oughta go out for quarterback. I didn't know a colored kid could—"

Whoops. I didn't mean to say that.

"Could what?" he asked, holding on to the ball and cocking his head.

I shrugged and looked around the yard like maybe somebody else had started that sentence and might be willing to finish it for us. When I looked back, the ball was comin' to me.

"Are you on a team?" he asked.

"I was co-first-string split end for the McWinkle Weasels last year. But junior high guys are a lot bigger, and my parents are making me wait a year to go out."

"Weasels?"

"It's some kind of small animal."

"Small? Is it mean?"

"I don't know. I hope so."

"I don't believe I'd want to be a weasel."

"So y'all don't have any teams or coaches at your school?" I asked him.

"Mrs. Langley makes us do jumping jacks sometimes."

"That's too bad, because you've got a great arm. I mean, you could play for the New York Giants."

He smiled big, like he was already playing quarterback for the New York Giants and knew what that felt like.

The Giants are my favorite pro team. Charlie Conerly went from quarterback at Ole Miss to quarterback for the Giants in the 1950s. My buddy Stokes told me it was Conerly who got them to wear gray pants with their red-and-blue jerseys like Ole Miss does.

"I mean, I never heard of a colored quarterback in the pros, but that doesn't mean—"

Dumb again. Double dumb.

"Maybe I'll be the first one," he said. He wasn't acting shy anymore. "I'm saving up my yard-work money, every cent, so I can buy some weights. Hand weights, barbells. Every kind of weight. I'll be one hundred percent muscle."

Willie Jane stuck her head out the door and yelled for us to come get our lunch.

"One more," I said. "Throw me one as far as you can throw it."

"Okay. One more."

I backed into Stokes's yard next door. Dee backed all the way into the street that runs up by the end of the house.

"Is this too far?" I called to him.

He shook his head, took a big breath, drew back, and let it fly.

"Holy smokes!"

That pass went so far it would have landed on the other side of Stokes's yard if I hadn't jumped as high as I could and caught it with the tip of my finger. It spun end over end and came down in the tall grass along the creek bank, hiding right at the edge. I reached for it.

And there was the snake.

• • •

Willie Jane is my other mama. When my real mama's gone to the beauty shop or the garden club or the country club or the Junior League, my other mama is always here. I'm supposed to mind her when she babysits us, but I can usually talk her into letting me stay up real late or eat a piece of pie before dinner. She's been spoiling me since I was born, Daddy says.

When I was Ginny Lynn's age, I'd sit by the ironing board and Willie Jane would tell me about how she grew up on a plantation outside Clarksdale. Her daddy was a sharecropper, which meant he had to give half his cotton to the man who owned the plantation and didn't get paid nearly enough for his own half. Her and her two brothers and her mama and daddy all lived in a three-room shotgun shack. They call it a shotgun shack because it's just rooms lined up in a row and if you fired a shotgun through the front door, the buckshot would go right out the back door.

She said one of her favorite things when she was a little girl was driving into town to buy hard candy and pinwheels, which didn't seem like much of a favorite thing to me. I told her one of my favorite things was when it rained with the sun still out, because I didn't see how that could happen. She said when the rain and the sunshine come at the same time, it means the devil is beating his wife. That explained it pretty well.

Willie Jane makes platefuls of Marguerites, which are crackers cooked with peanut butter on them and marshmallows melted on top. It's the best snack ever invented. She makes lunch and supper for us, too. She cooks the best fried chicken and mashed potatoes you ever tasted. Spoon some chicken gravy on those potatoes and it's good enough to make a hound dog hug a rabbit. That's what my papaw says.

When I was little, I mixed different colors of Play-Doh together until it was brown and rolled it up and snuck behind Willie Jane and yelled "Snake!" and slung it on the ironing board. She jumped and whooped and hollered, "Child! I almost fell out!" She chased me to my room, and I hid under the bed where she couldn't reach me. We were both laughing the whole time.

Willie Jane hates snakes, but I don't think she's really scared of them. She's not scared of much. Which is good, because I about peed in my pants when I almost grabbed that thing by the creek. I'm probably old enough to take care of snakes myself, but I've been running to my other mama for help my whole life, and I'm not ready to give it up.

I had to think about my sisters. What if Farish had been the one who found that snake? She probably would have tried to pick it up.

Dee and I ran to the house. Farish was eating her pimiento cheese sandwich in the kitchen. Willie Jane was still ironing in the playroom.

"Snake!" we yelled. "Willie Jane . . . snake . . . down at the creek! You gotta help us!"

"We were throwing . . . the ball." Dee took a big breath. "And Trip leaned down and . . . there it was!"

"Lyin' real still," I panted. "So it can jump up and bite!"

Willie Jane set down her iron. "What kinda snake?"

"The kind that makes you sick to look at it," I told her.

"It's light brown and dark brown with a big triangle head," Dee said.

"And y'all didn't mess with it?"

"Unh-unh," I said. "I did what the snake man at school told us: Take three steps back and run!"

"Where's the ball?" asked Farish, gnawing on her sandwich with her eyes buggin' out.

"Still down there," I said, "where do you think?"

"I'm gonna go get it," she said.

"No you're not!" I told her.

"Farish, you stay here and look after Ginny Lynn," said Willie Jane. "Boys, y'all come on. I'll get the hoe out of the shed."

Farish won't mind anybody unless it's something she already wants to do or you tell her five times. She dragged Ginny Lynn to the patio so she could watch. Ginny Lynn didn't want to watch. Farish held her hand and tried to sound like Mama, shushing and whispering that everything was going to be okay.

Willie Jane got the hoe and we started down the yard. She waved it around as we went, in case she had to use it quick. That snake might have started crawling toward the house. We kept our eyes on the ground and stepped as quiet as we could.

I pointed to the spot and we walked closer. There was the ball. But no snake.

"It's gone," I whispered.

"He's still around somewhere," Willie Jane said. "Or his friend is." She looked like she couldn't wait to chop up some snake salad with that hoe.

I snatched up the ball and almost fell over trying to back up quick. We walked along the bank from one end to the other, one slow step at a time, Willie Jane swishing the hoe through the tall grass. Then we looked for it over in Mr. Pinky's yard across the creek. No snake.

"It must have slithered off," Willie Jane said. She leaned on the hoe and squinted at me and Dee. It made me so nervous, I started shifting my feet. "That is, if there *was* a snake in the first place."

"There was!" we said together.

"Y'all better not have stopped my ironin' so you could fugaboo me about some snake."

"We saw it, Mama!"

"We saw it, Willie Jane, I swear!"

It wasn't fair she didn't believe us.

"You better have." She headed back to the house, using the hoe like a walking stick. "Here I am swingin' a hoe around, my hip all stove up from vacuumin' and . . ."

We begged her to believe us all the way up the yard. She finally turned around before she went inside: "No mowin' by the creek, Dee, you hear me? Don't mess around down there. It's liable to come back."

Everything has pretty much stayed the same my whole life. I've always lived at 5445 Oak Lane Drive, the house on the corner; my phone number has always been Emerson-68692; I went to McWinkle Elementary the whole way and I'll go to Donelson Junior High the whole way. I've added some sisters. That's about all. When nothing ever changes and everybody seems okay, you don't ask a lot of questions. But I'm starting to think the grown-ups don't have everything figured out.

I've always gone to Broadview Baptist Church, and I'm always *going* to Broadview Baptist Church. If it's Sunday morning, it's time for Sunday School; if it's Sunday night, it's time for Training Union; if it's Wednesday night, it's time for Prayer Meeting. Not to mention church softball, church basketball, Vacation Bible School, and a buttload of other "opportunities for worship and fellowship." If the doors are open, we're halfway down, right side of the middle section.

I had spent the night at Stokes's house, and we stayed up real late, but I still had to jump up and run home and get ready for Sunday School. Stokes's mom had taken us to see *Goldfinger* at the Capri, and it was all I could think about. When I told Mama, she said, "Doris Cargyle is a wonderful woman, but she and I obviously have very different ideas about what kinds of movies a twelve-year-old boy should watch." It bothered me in a way I can't really explain that she and Mrs. Cargyle had very different ideas. When I was little, the grown-ups agreed about everything.

It was hot in that Sunday School room, the kind of dry heat that stops up your nose and makes your back itch, and those rickety metal chairs were hard to sit in and people kept squeaking them. Plus, Mr. Dukes's fingernails were so dirty, it was hard to listen to today's lesson. What the heck was he doing before church, working on cars? He's all bald-headed and creased in the face, too. I felt bad for thinking about it, though. Mr. Dukes could help his fingernails but not his face. I sat up straighter and tried to pay better attention so God wouldn't make *me* bald and creased when I got old.

Mr. Dukes told us God watches everything we do and keeps track of how many times we sin. He said if we bump our heads or stump our toes, that's God saying, "Cut out that sinnin', or else." I guess it must be true, but I don't especially want God watching me go to the bathroom.

Today's lesson was about Noah. Mr. Dukes told us about the flood and how after forty days, Noah sent out a dove to see if the water had gone down, and when the dove never came back, they were finally able to get off that ark, which had to smell pretty terrible if you think about it. And then God promised not to drown everybody again, and that's why we have rainbows.

"Now, boys and girls, we need to talk about Noah's sons, who fathered all the peoples of the earth," said Mr. Dukes. "And the cursing of Ham." Cursing ham felt about right to me. Especially cold ham with fat all in it.

"Let's everybody put your Bible in your lap," he said. "Ready? Genesis chapter nine, verse twenty-five!"

I've won the most Bible drills this fall and obviously turned to Genesis 9:25 faster than anybody else, and stood up *before* Donnie Rogers, even if he yelled "Got it!" Mr. Dukes didn't know who was really first because he was too busy shushing Ramona McLowry. Ramona does have some long, thick blond hair. I'm not saying I like her or anything.

Mr. Dukes should have been shushing Tim and Tom Bethune and their buddies in the back. They're the oldest members of the junior high Sunday School class and think they're too cool to be in it and never shut up.

"'Cursed be Canaan; a slave of slaves shall he be to his brothers,'" read Mr. Dukes. "'He also said, Blessed by the Lord my God be Shem; and let Canaan be his slave. God enlarge Japheth, and let him dwell in the tents of Shem; and let Canaan be his slave.'"

I raised my hand. "I thought you said *Ham* got cursed. What's that about Canaan?"

"Canaan was Ham's son. It's the same thing."

"Well, why would Noah curse him?"

"Ham walked into Noah's tent and saw Noah naked."

"On purpose?"

"I believe it was an accident."

"That doesn't seem like much of a reason to curse somebody, if you ask me."

Mr. Dukes looked at the back wall and acted like he hadn't heard me. "Now, boys and girls, if y'all will look on over at chapter ten, you'll see the names of all of Ham's sons. Somebody tell me what it says there in verse six."

"Cush, Egypt, Phut, and Canaan," said singsongy Cathy Hathcock.

"That's right. And who can tell me where Egypt is?"

"Africa," I said.

"That's right, son. Africa." He looked from one side of the room to the other, like he wanted it to sink in real good that Egypt was in Africa. "Where the nigra slaves came from."

"I thought you said *Canaan* got cursed," I said.

Mr. Dukes squinted at me. He doesn't like too many questions.

"We are learning what the Bible has to say about Africa."

Then it was time for big church. Everybody scraped and squeaked their chairs and headed for the door. I was confused.

"Mr. Dukes, are you saying that since slaves came from Africa, slaves are okay with God?"

"I'm not saying anything, son. I'm letting my Bible do the talking."

Sometimes Dr. Mercer's sermons are about the same Bible verses we read in Sunday School, so I was hoping to hear more about Noah and Ham and Africa. Maybe Dr. Mercer could clear some of that up for me. But he started on something else. When he got to the part he always gets to about how we are all unworthy sinners who need saving from everlasting damnation, I knew I wasn't going to hear any more about Africa today. I don't know why I thought I might. Dr. Mercer never talks about colored people.

I started doodling on the bulletin and drew a big round face with no hair and creases on it and eyebrows slanting up toward each other and a wriggly mouth that curved up just a little on both ends, like a smile you would make if you accidentally let out a big one in the sanctuary. Farish saw what I drew and laughed till she had to pretend she was having a coughing fit. I wrote, "Hi, boys and girls, I'm Mr. Fart!" under the face, and she had to cough some more.

Daddy looked over and saw what I drew, and he started coughing, too. Mama snatched it out of my lap.

On the way to meet Meemaw and Papaw for lunch, I told Mama about today's Sunday School lesson and asked her if she'd ever heard Dr. Mercer talk about colored people. She said she never had. I asked her why, and she said she didn't know. Daddy took his eyes off the road and raised his eyebrows at her like she did too know.

"So you *do* know?" I asked her.

"It's complicated, pal," Daddy said. "Let's talk about it later."

I nodded, but I still wondered about Dr. Mercer. He was the preacher, after all. My history teacher, Miss Hooper, talks about them. Miss Hooper is the prettiest teacher at the whole school, you can ask anybody. She has big eyes, greenish-bluish, like the water at Pensacola, and long blond hair piled up, and man, she is stacked. Her whole body is kind of perfect. She's from Jackson but she has a boyfriend in law school way up in Maryland or somewhere. That might not be true. I've never seen him.

She told us about Medgar Evers, how he tried so hard to help colored people be able to vote and got shot in his driveway for doing it. And she told us how three Freedom Riders from up North got killed in Philadelphia last June for trying to help colored people vote. I thought Philadelphia was only in Pennsylvania, but it turns out we have a Philadelphia here.

Sadie Rae Jenkins raised her hand and said it was a shame the way everybody hates Mississippi, and she didn't have any KKK in her neighborhood.

I was thinking, What do you know, Prissy-Pants Jenkins said something right for a change. I don't want to live in a place everybody hates, and I don't see why they should hate us, at least not all of us. I don't have any KKK in my neighborhood either. If somebody from Philadelphia, Pennsylvania, visited my neighborhood and my school and my church, he wouldn't find a bunch of mean white people trying to hurt colored people. They might say things about colored people sometimes, but people here are nice.

But Miss Hooper told Sadie Rae it wasn't just a few Klansmen giving Mississippi a bad name. If a colored person couldn't vote without somebody getting killed, *Mississippi* was giving Mississippi a bad name. She said the hardest thing for her or anybody to understand about our state is how people who are so warm and kind and full of "Southern hospitality," and who would never outright hurt colored people, can be so full of prejudice against them.

"But it doesn't matter how people feel about it, it's the *law*," Nancy Harper said. "Public places have to be shared by everybody. The South has to integrate, especially the schools." She says it "schoo-ulls." She moved down from Ohio last spring and acts like she owns the place. She also says "look-it" and "you guys" instead of "y'all."

"No we do not," Bobby Watson said, crossing his arms. A couple of guys applauded.

"*Brown versus Board of Education*, 1954. Look it up," Nancy said.

"Well, this is 1964," Bobby said.

"Nancy is right, Bobby," Miss Hooper said.

"The Civil Rights Act, July 2, 1964," Nancy said.

"Oh, shut up," Bobby said. "Not you, Miss Hooper."

Miss Hooper said the South has no choice but to integrate schools and try to get rid of its prejudice, and to do that it will have to get rid of its ignorance and guilt.

"Guilt about what?" Bobby asked.

"That's a good question. I believe there is still a lot of guilt about slavery in this culture, and about Jim Crow, even though the laws have been in effect for almost one hundred years."

She told us that Jim Crow laws were named after a white guy who painted his face black in the 1800s and called himself "Jim Crow." He did musical shows mocking colored people and making them seem lazy and stupid, not even real people. So the "real" people named segregation laws after him. And segregation was just another kind of slavery.

She pointed to everybody in the class. "It's up to you to think about what kind of state you want to live in. It's up to each one of you to improve your state's image."

I don't know what she expects us to do. We're twelve.

Daddy says prejudice is one reason he's thinking about moving us to Kansas City. His friend from medical school has offered him a job at a clinic up there. Mama says she cannot bear the thought of "uprooting" our family like that, and it would just kill her parents, especially her mother.

When we got to the country club, Mama looked at me. "Don't bring up anything about Dr. Mercer and colored people at the dinner table." Like I didn't know that already.

We usually have Sunday dinner at noon with Meemaw and Papaw, either at their house or the country club. "Meemaw Table Rules" are the same wherever we eat. The food is great, especially at Meemaw's house, where it's fried chicken or roast beef or pork chops, garden tomatoes, baby butter beans, mashed potatoes, fried okra, squash casserole, English peas, homemade rolls, cornbread, peach cobbler, Meemaw's world-famous chocolate milk shakes, all kinds of stuff. But the rules are a pain. On the way home from Sunday dinner me and Farish always start crackin' up about something or other—we're just that glad to get away from Meemaw Table Rules.

Meemaw and Papaw were waiting in the downstairs restaurant, the Golliwog. Church lasts forever, and by the time we get to the club, my stomach is making outer-space noises and shrunk to the size of a peanut. Everybody knows us, and they all smile and wave when we walk in and we have to stop and chat at a couple of tables before we can sit down. Then, right when we're ready to order, one of Daddy's patients will come over, and when she finally leaves, some people from the church will come over, and I have to keep smiling until they leave, and then, if we're lucky, we can finally get some food.

Me and Farish always order the cheeseburger with sautéed onions and greasy log fries and ice cream pie. All the food is good. And all the people eating it are white. And all the people bringing it are colored, except the manager, Mr. Lonnie. Today, I started wondering why that is.

The waiters smile when they come to the table. Papaw always teases them and they always laugh. They seem to really like him. They seem to like everybody. But I was watching Shelby, the tall one with the white hair who's been here ever since I can remember. Does he really like everybody? I wonder if he's thinking, You better leave me a big tip, whitey-butt, if I have to smile this much.

Mama says Papaw's bank that he started is the third-biggest in the state of Mississippi. I asked her if that meant he was the third-richest man in Mississippi, and she said him and Meemaw were "very comfortable." I asked her why, in that case, it was so hard for him to hand over a nickel for a pack of Juicy Fruit. She said the Great Depression taught him the value of a nickel. So I don't know what kind of tips he's leaving Shelby.

I knew I couldn't talk about colored people, but I wanted to talk about *Goldfinger* so bad, I was afraid to open my mouth for fear of it slippin' out. That would be violating Meemaw Table Rule Number One: *Do not talk about movies.* Even if you just watched the best movie you ever saw in your life, you cannot mention it at the table because Meemaw thinks movies are a "stench in the nostrils of the Lord," and doesn't know why they are allowed to be shown to the public, what with all the violence and women running around half-naked—which I say is the reason to go see 'em.

Rule Number Two is *Do not talk about playing cards.*

Even if it's Go Fish. Playing cards leads to gambling and gambling is sinful. After we got back from *Goldfinger,* me and Stokes played Battle for three hours straight, which was a new record. Couldn't mention it.

Rule Number Three is *Do not talk about dancing.* Dancing is bad. I hate going to school dances, so it's no problem not to talk about it.

Rule Number Four is *Pretty much do not talk about anything.* Except school and church.

I couldn't have gotten a word in edgewise anyway, with Papaw carrying on like he was, about the country "goin' to hell in a handbasket" and rock 'n' roll being music for "yay-hos."

He asked me if I had any thoughts on the subject of rock 'n' roll, and I said I was too busy eating to have any thoughts. Everybody laughed. But by the time they brought the ice cream pie, I couldn't stand it anymore.

"Have y'all ever heard of James Bond, agent double-oh-seven?"

Mama glared at me, and I went back to my pie.

When everybody was finished, me and Papaw and Daddy left the "womenfolk"—that's a Papaw word—and went out to the patio. Daddy said he'd see if there were a couple of guys in the locker room looking for a foursome. Papaw lit up an Old Gold and said he'd be right there.

"It's turning into a real nice day," I said.

"Yeah!" said Papaw. He likes to give everything a big "Yeah!" I told him, like I always do, that I didn't know why he liked cigarettes, and he said, like he always does, "It's a filthy habit, son. I only smoke a few."

He propped one foot on the curb, rested his cigarette arm on it, tilted his Sunday hat against the sun, and looked down at the golf course like he owned it— which he kind of does, I guess, since he was one of the people who started this country club.

Then I said, "Papaw, can you imagine anybody naming their kid Ham? I mean, why not Pot Roast, right?"

"Ham?" He just looked at me.

My heart was going to town all of a sudden. I had to just come out and ask.

"Papaw, do you think the Bible says white people are supposed to be the boss of colored people?"

"No, son, I don't. I know there's some that do believe that. But I don't."

"Have you ever thought Shelby and all them might get tired of waitin' on white people's tables all the time? I bet sometimes they wish they could sit down and eat."

He laughed.

"It's paid work." He said it "woik." He says "woik" for "work," and "Hawaya" for "Hawaii" and "Colyarada" for "Colorado." He and Meemaw are both from the Delta, where all the cotton gets planted. I never met anybody from the Delta who said his *r*s.

"We pay the Negroes good, and most of 'em do a good job. Everybody's gettin' along fine." He patted me on the shoulder. "Shelby gets plenty to eat, don't worry."

"You think they're happy?"

"Do they seem unhappy to you?"

"No. I've just been thinking about it."

He patted me again.

"You know, your meemaw and I give a lot of money to the church to help the poor people, here and in foreign countries. The maid gets her bonus every Christmas and Meemaw gives her extra clothes for her boys and girls and such as that. It's all our Christian duty to help the coloreds." He sounded kind of formal all of a sudden.

"What if there was a colored person who wasn't poor and wanted to join the country club? Would y'all let him?"

"Well, you know, Trip, people tend to want to socialize with their own kind. They have their schools and churches and clubs and so on, and we have ours, and it's probably best to keep it all separate. That's the way we can best help 'em. Anyway, I don't 'spect there's a Negro around here could afford it."

"Well, what if he was real hungry and just wanted to sit down and eat in the Golliwog? Would that be all right?"

He looked at me like he could not understand why in the world I would ask such a question.

"I tell ya what, you bring me a morally upstanding Negro who's hungry and wants to eat in the Golliwog, and I'll buy him lunch, okay?"

He smiled and flicked the stub of his cigarette into the grass. I always worry he'll catch it on fire, but he never does. "You think we got all that straight? I 'spect your daddy's wondering where I am."

When we got home, I looked up the word "golli-wog" in the dictionary. It turns out a golliwog is a doll with a black face or a white person who paints his face black. And "wog" is a word making fun of colored people. They named the dining room downstairs after the waiters? Are they saying this is where you can eat in the less fancy room and pretend you're a colored person, who always eats in a less fancy room? I thought about Dee, and calling it the Golliwog seemed nothing but mean.

Stokes said that snake must have been a cottonmouth. He said maybe we couldn't find it at the creek because it was already in the house under my bed. I can't be-lieve he thinks I would fall for that story. There is no snake under my bed, I checked.

Friday night, I stayed up reading Greek myths,

mostly the one about Jason and the Argonauts and the quest for the golden fleece. That's my favorite. On Saturday, the guys were coming over for a game right after lunch. I jumped out of bed late and went straight to the porch to check the weather.

It was a bright day with a cool breeze, and I thought I smelled corn dogs and elephant ears. It was just wishful smellin'. The fair doesn't get here till next week, and it's a long way from my house. Farish and Ginny Lynn love the fair so much, they made up a silly song about it: "The fair, the fair, it's everywhere! So beware!"

I took a deep breath full of cool breeze and corn dogs and elephant ears and stretched out my arms like an Argonaut smelling a miracle.

"The perfume of the gods!" I shouted.

And there was Dee, raking by the rose bed. He half smiled at me like, "Hello, weird shouting kid."

I kind of waved and went inside.

"What's Dee doin' in the front yard?" I asked Willie Jane. "It looks like he's just getting started on it."

"We just got here, sleepyhead. The Buick wouldn't start."

"But everybody's coming over to play football in less than an hour. He's not gonna be finished in time."

"You'll have to talk to your mama about that."

I thought about grabbing another rake so I could help Dee hurry up, but I decided against it. Then I thought maybe a Coca-Cola would help him go faster. I took him one and he acted like he didn't want it but drank it down anyway and went right back to work. I wanted to tell him to quit being so slow and careful, but I couldn't figure out how to say it.

When Mama came back from the grocery store, I asked her if Dee could stop working and let me and the guys have our football game. She said we would just have to wait, that Dee needed to finish what he started, and we could play down at Calvin Stubbs's house if we were that impatient.

"Calvin's yard is no good," I told her.

"Y'all can find another yard somewhere."

"Everybody else's is too small or has too many trees."

"Y'all can figure it out."

"Well, I don't see why he couldn't go work in the back while we're playin' and finish the front when we're through."

"Because he did the back last weekend, and mainly because I said so."

"Well, okay . . . but he's looking awfully tired out there today. Have you seen him? I bet he could use a break. A long break."

"What? Dee's okay, isn't he?" She looked out the window and brought her hand to her throat. She ran to the kitchen and got a Coca-Cola.

Dee took it from her and drank the whole thing quick like a soldier, handed her the empty bottle, and snapped his hand back on the rake. When she came back into the house, Mama told Willie Jane that her boy was surely a hard worker, and she hoped he wasn't getting too worn out.

"Oh, he's fine, Miz Westbrook," Willie Jane said. "Dee's tough. And the good Lord knows we need the money."

I've asked Mama before why Willie Jane doesn't call her Virginia or at least *Miz* Virginia, as long as they've known each other. Everybody else calls her Virginia. She says the people who work for you are not "everybody" and that's just the way it is.

But Willie Jane doesn't just work for us. She's my other mama.

"I don't have anything to give him when he wants to go see a show at the Alamo," Willie Jane said.

The Alamo is the colored people's theater. White people go to the Paramount or the Capri or the Lamar downtown.

I asked Mama why Willie Jane has to wear a white uniform to work in our house when we're not a hotel or something, and Mama said it's the proper thing for maids to wear. She said some people have a separate bathroom for the maid like Meemaw and Papaw and at least we don't do that. When you walk up the steps from the garage to Meemaw and Papaw's back door, there's a little bathroom at the top, with a little commode that looks like it's covered with rust or something.

While me and Mama were eating egg and olive sandwiches, I told her she needed to pay Willie Jane more. She laughed and said she had already gotten that message today.

"You really ought to, though," I said.

I downed my milk and checked the clock. The guys would be here any minute. I ran outside with another Coca-Cola, but Dee waved me away when he saw it.

Oakwood used to be three streets in a row with a creek winding through them and woods on both ends. Now they're chopping down all the trees and adding on new streets. I miss playing in those woods. Once when we were playing hide-and-seek, I climbed so high in a pine tree, everybody gave up trying to find me and went home to supper.

The two best sounds in the neighborhood are the tinkle of the Popsicle truck and the buzz of the foggin' machine that sprays for mosquitoes. We used to stop whatever we were doing and run, get right in the middle of that fog where we couldn't see anything but white and spin around till we were dizzy. It smells pretty sweet. You wouldn't think it could kill mosquitoes.

Stokes lives right next door, and he's my best friend, but I've got lots of others in Oakwood. When there's nothing else to do, three or four of us get together and walk all over the neighborhood, sometimes even all the way to the Tote-Sum for an Orange Crush or a candy bar.

Mrs. Sitwell across the street always waves.

Mr. Nelson lives across the corner, and him and Mrs. Nelson are always outside working on their yard. They wave and say, "What you been up to?" and "How your folks getting along?" and stuff like that.

Old Mr. Hollingsworth is always rocking on his porch and him and me always have the same conversation:

"Hey there, Trip!"

"Hey, Mr. Hollingsworth."

"How's your daddy doin'?"

"He's doin' fine."

"Your daddy is a fine man."

"Yessir."

"Did you know he delivered every one of my grandbabies?"

"He did?"

"He sure did." And he smiles and shakes his head.

Mr. Pinky lives across the creek behind us. His garden is full of all kinds of vegetables, and he brings us big sacks of tomatoes and cucumbers and says to come pick anything we want. His real name is Mr. Sanderford, but people call him Pinky because his bald head is so pink from the sun shining on it when he works in his garden. Mrs. Pinky is real nice, too.

When I told Stokes today's game would have to be moved, he got pretty mad. There are lots of big yards in Oakwood, but nobody has a better yard for playing football than mine. The trees leave a great big oval from the rose bed to the driveway. You just have to watch out for the sidewalk in the middle and you can't mind it too much if a low-hanging branch intercepts a pass now and then. And you can't hurt Mama's roses.

"Can't you get your mom to make the yard boy come back later?" asked Stokes.

"What do you think I've been tryin' to do?"

"You could tell him you've seen a whole lot more snakes in the front yard, like the one y'all saw in the back. They hate snakes."

"That would be completely not true."

"So?"

Stokes is more likely than anybody I know to make something up. On the day he moved in next door, when we were both five years old, he told me his daddy was a werewolf. He said he had seen his daddy change one night when the moon was full, that he got hair all over his body and his face turned into a wolf face and he howled and busted out the front door and went looking for people to devour.

For the next week, I was afraid to go outside after

supper in case Stokes's dad was out there. I couldn't figure out how to bring it up with my parents, but finally I had to ask Mama about it, and she said Stokes was just having fun with me, and it was only a story, and I should tell him my daddy was a vampire. I tried it, but Stokes never would believe me.

Stokes is taller than me by about three inches, even though we're both in seventh grade, and his hair is a lot darker, his face is longer, and he has more freckles. He's thicker than me, too. The only way I've ever beaten him in wrestling is with my scissors hold. If I can get him in a scissors, it's all over. One time I held him in a scissors for about five minutes, laughing the whole time, not being a very good sport, I guess. He got so mad that when he finally said "uncle" and I let him loose, he slugged me in the face and went home. I would have hit him back, but I was too surprised.

The next day he told me he was sorry he had lost his temper. That was the only time we've ever had a real fight. It's not my fault that I have superhuman leg abilities. Daddy says it makes up for the fact that I don't have muscles anywhere else. Ha, ha. I do so.

We passed the ball back and forth on the side of the yard where Dee wasn't working, and talked about where to move the game and couldn't come up with a better yard than Calvin's.

It's usually me and Stokes, Calvin, Andy, and maybe

some other guys. We let Kenny Tutwiler play, but he's little and always has a runny nose and gets it on the ball. Stokes is a pretty good quarterback. He can out-run everybody except me.

My favorite team would have to be Stokes at quarter-back, me going out for passes, and Calvin snapping the ball and blocking because even though he's only eleven, he's as wide as a table. Let's just say Calvin likes his Twinkies. Andy's medium tall, skinny, and fast, and probably loves to play more than anybody. He comes around every Saturday chewing on a straw, spinning a football, and looking for a game.

Before they got to be teenagers, the Bethune twins would play. Now they think they're too cool to talk to seventh graders. Fine with me. They were always complaining about something, saying it was a com-plete pass when they had scooped it off the ground, or that they had crossed the goal line without getting touched with two hands when they did get touched. The rule is you have to count "one Mississippi, two Mississippi" up to five, loud and not too fast, before you can rush the quarterback. They always said I short-ened it up to "one Miss'ippi, two Miss'ippi. . . ." Well, heck, that's how people in Miss'ippi say it. Maybe they don't know that because they're from Louisiana and pull for the LSU Tigers and won't shut up about it. But they don't want to talk about how Ole Miss has beaten LSU the last two years—and they're gonna do it again this Halloween, bet you anything.

The Bethunes live next door to Mr. Pinky, and I heard him tell Daddy, "Them boys ride their bikes up in my front yard like they think it's theirs. I never know when a firecracker will go off in my garden late at night. Cherry bombs, sometimes. Hurts the vegetables."

Mr. Bethune is nice, though. One time, Tim showed me his World War II model aircraft carriers, and Mr. Bethune explained all the different parts of the ships. At church, he always gives me a "Chinese haircut," which means he rubs his knuckles real fast on the top of my head, and calls me a "wisenheimer," which means "smart aleck." He learned it from the Germans during World War II. I told Daddy I wanted a model aircraft kit like one of Tim's, and he said that was the first time he'd heard of a Bethune boy building something instead of tearing it up.

I stood in the middle of the yard and Stokes was on the driveway. He threw one over my head, and it rolled all the way to where Dee was working. Dee picked up the ball and smiled, and all of a sudden I felt bad that I hadn't asked him to throw it with us, the way we had thrown it last week.

"Where'd you get them pearly whites, boy?" Stokes yelled to him in a colored-person accent like a lot of white people do when they talk to them. I'm pretty sure the colored person can tell.

Dee reared back and threw a pass that hit Stokes so hard in the gut he couldn't hang on to it.

"Same place you got yours, I reckon." Dee smiled and picked up his rake.

Stokes stared at Dee, like first of all, he couldn't believe Dee could throw a pass like that, and second, did this colored kid just hurt his stomach on purpose? Then he picked it up and passed it to me real quick, pretending like nothing had happened. But something had.

"Watch this," I told Stokes. I walked over to Dee and handed him the ball.

"Tell you what, Dee, I'm gonna run all the way into Stokes's yard and when I get w-a-a-a-y down there, see if you can hit me with a pass. Okay?"

"Come on, Trip!" Stokes was holding out his arms like I had gone crazy.

"Ready, Dee?"

"Ready."

I got into my stance.

"Hut one! Hut two! Hut three!"

I tore across the yard and cut to the middle and tore across Stokes's yard and when I looked back, here came the ball, floating right into my hands.

"Touchdown!" I held up my arms in the signal.

Dee smiled big. Stokes looked annoyed.

"Hey, Dee, how 'bout you stop working for a while and throw with us," I said.

"He can't throw with us!" Stokes was yelling and whispering at the same time.

"Why not?" I said.

"He's the yard boy!"

I spun the ball up in the air and caught it and tried to act all normal and relaxed.

"Come on, Dee!" I yelled. "Whatcha say?"

Dee looked a little bit scared, but he nodded.

I walked to the street to get the most distance between everybody. Stokes stayed on the driveway. I threw to Dee. He reached back and let it fly and hit Stokes in the breadbasket again. Stokes let it drop. He could have caught that one. He picked it up and lateraled it to me and started walking back to his house.

"What are you doing?" I said.

He shook his head.

"Come on! What's your hang-up?" Stokes was acting like he was caught on something invisible and couldn't get loose.

"What's *your* hang-up?" he said.

"Don't spaz out on me, okay?"

"*You're* a spaz."

I threw the ball to him and he caught it, and then he squinted at Dee down at the other side of the yard and heaved it so hard, Dee had to backpedal and jump for it. But he brought it down.

"Nice catch!" I yelled.

Mama's always saying I do things too hard. I play too hard. I sleep too hard. I argue with her and Daddy too hard. I tend to go overboard in general. Sometimes I even do homework too hard, like when I wrote three times as many pages as anybody else on my *Moby-Dick* paper and made a visual aid of a Popsicle-stick ship, when the teacher didn't even ask for visual aids, and it had a harpooned whale tied to the side, filled up with blubber made out of Crisco and red food coloring. Today, maybe I wanted to play football too hard.

"Hey, Dee, you wanna play in our game when the rest of the guys get here?"

He looked confused.

"See ya," Stokes said.

"Wait, wait, Stokes, wait, just listen. . . ."

"He can't play a game with us, Trip! For crying out loud!" He was yell-whispering again and looking at me like I was crazy.

"Listen, if Dee's playing football with us, he's not raking the yard, and if he's not raking the yard, we don't have to go over to Calvin's and play in his crummy yard and put up with his whole family."

"Yeah," said Stokes. "And what's everybody gonna think?"

"Who cares what they think?"

"They won't do it."

"So we'll talk 'em into it. My daddy played with colored kids in New Orleans growing up. And he worked with colored doctors and doctored on colored soldiers at an army hospital in the Korean War."

"Well, this ain't the Korean War."

"I tell you what, I want a guy with an arm like that on my team. I don't care if he's black, white, or purple."

Stokes thought for a second.

"He can throw a football, I'll grant you that," said Stokes. He learned "I'll grant you" somewhere, and lately he's always granting me things. "But I don't know. . . ."

"Will you just think about it?"

Dee had gone back to work while we were talking. I asked him again to play with us.

"My mama brought me over here to take care of the yard," he said. "I expect that's what I oughta do."

"Let's go ask her."

We left Stokes standing there, still thinking it over.

Willie Jane shook her head at first. Then she said, "Dee, you really want to play in their game?"

He didn't act as sure about it as I wanted him to, but he nodded.

"You sure?"

"Yes, ma'am."

"All right then. Trip, go see what ya mama says."

I took a deep breath and went in there. I didn't know what Mama would say, because I'm not really sure what she thinks about colored people and white people doing stuff together. Also, she doesn't like to be interrupted when she's polishing her fingers and toes. She wanted to know why I was bothering her again. Dee had to finish the yard.

"But we don't just want Dee to quit working on the yard. We want him to play with us."

"*Play* with you?"

"Yes, ma'am. Be on somebody's team. I bet Daddy would say he could."

She looked all around the room like there might be somebody there she could ask about this. Then she got this look on her face like she was about to do something naughty.

"Well, I . . . I think it will be fine. It will be *fine* if Dee plays football with y'all. He can finish the yard when the game's over."

Me and Stokes and Dee passed it around, spreading out from each other as far as we could and still be in the yard, not talking a whole lot. Once we got into a rhythm with the ball, Stokes seemed to quit caring who he was throwing it to.

Andy showed up. His legs are always scraped up from playing in shorts. Calvin and little Kenny Tutwiler came together half a minute later.

"All right," I told them, "I'm a captain and Stokes is a captain."

"And I pick first," said Stokes.

I didn't argue. Mama says "choose your battles," and there were bound to be worse battles before this game was over.

They had been wondering why this colored kid was standing around, but when he lined up like he was waiting to get picked, they were really confused. There was his rake lying over by the rose bed, why wasn't he using it? That's what they wanted to say, but nobody did. They just looked at each other. Kenny wiped his nose with one hand and raised his other hand.

"You can't volunteer for a team, Kenny. You have to wait and get picked," I told him.

"I have a question."

"What is it?"

He pointed at Dee. "Did y'all hire him to be the referee or somethin'?"

"No, he's gonna play with us. This is Dee."

Calvin and Andy mumbled their names at Dee. Kenny stood there scratching. Stokes looked at the ground.

Andy asked if we could all huddle up for a second, meaning all of us but Dee. He wasn't trying to be mean about it. I felt bad, though, leaving Dee out.

You could tell he would just as soon go back to raking. I caught his eye and held up my hand in a signal that he should be patient and everything was going to be all right.

"Dee is good," I whispered to them in the huddle. "He's *real* good."

"He's a nig—" said Andy.

"Don't say that," I said.

"He's a *Ne-gro*," said Andy, making his mouth real big. Calvin and Kenny laughed. Stokes still looked at the ground.

"I'll tell y'all something, I don't care." And when I said it, I knew it was the truth. All these people worried about whether somebody is white or colored, that didn't mean I had to worry about it. Not if I didn't want to. "He's Willie Jane's son."

"So?" said Andy.

"So Willie Jane is one of the family."

"Does that make y'all brothers?" said Andy, and now they really laughed.

"Is that what you're saying, Trip?" said Calvin. "Colored boy here is your brother?"

"I'm saying wait till you see him throw a pass. Dee can play some football, can't he, Stokes?"

Stokes finally looked up and nodded and said, "Dee can play. And if he's playin' instead of workin', we can have our field."

Good ol' Stokes.

"I don't know about this," said Kenny, trying to sound like the older guys.

"Play in Calvin's yard if you want to," I told them.

"You comin' with us?" Calvin asked me.

"I'm stayin' right here."

"Can we use your ball?" asked Kenny.

Andy's ball is shorter and fatter than my Spalding and harder to throw.

"I'm stayin' right here, and my ball is stayin' with me."

Everybody just stood there awhile with their faces scrunched.

Then Stokes said, "Okay, my team is the Nighthawks."

"We're the Rebels," I said.

Stokes picked Andy. I picked Dee. Then Stokes picked Calvin, which left Kenny for my team. Fine with me. I'd have the best quarterback–split end combo in town. All Kenny had to do was snap the ball and try to get in the way of whoever was rushing long enough for Dee to throw it to me.

I went over the rules for Dee: Two-handed touch, because our moms don't like tackle; you have to run for the extra point, but it just counts one, like a kick;

if a tree blocks a kick or a pass, you run the play again. The first team to score five touchdowns wins.

Andy flipped his buffalo nickel, and I called heads. Heads it was. The Nighthawks lined up on the rose-bed side, and the Rebels lined up on the driveway side. Me and Dee played deep to receive the kick.

"Ready?" I said, so he would look at me and see me smiling and know that we were about to have some fun.

He nodded but he didn't smile back. He had the same determined face as when he was doing yard work.

I wondered if I had goofed up. Was I forcing Dee to play with all these white boys when he didn't really want to? Maybe he didn't know how to tell me he didn't want to. I had to admit he looked way out of place. And he must have felt it.

I was about to ask him if he'd rather go back to raking, but here came Calvin running at the tee like an angry bear. Calvin always brings the tee he got for Christmas last year, which gives him automatic kicking rights. The trouble is he can't kick worth a flip.

Thunk!

It barely got across the sidewalk and dribbled on the ground for about ten yards. Stokes grabbed it and flew by us, all the way to the end zone.

"Touchdown!" yelled Andy.

"You can't receive your own kickoff!" I screamed.

"Onside kick! Onside kick!" yelled Andy. He and Calvin were laughing like the luckiest, best thing in the world had just happened.

Stokes stood on the driveway and held the ball up for everybody to admire and yelled for us to come down there and line up for the extra point. "If the ball goes at least ten yards, it's a free ball. Anybody can pick it up," said Andy, which was true, now that I thought about it, but they didn't have to laugh so much.

"It's not like Calvin kicked it that way on purpose," I said.

"I did too," fibbed Calvin.

We lined up for the extra point and they ran it in and it was Nighthawks 7, Rebels 0.

I stood up close for the kickoff. Kenny stood at midfield and Dee stood all the way back. Calvin actually got it in the air this time. Dee caught it and took off and Stokes got two hands on him around midfield.

On our first play from scrimmage Dee took the snap from Kenny; then Kenny backed up and tried to block for Dee. I ran out for a pass, about twenty yards down the sideline. Dee took a few steps back, planted his feet, and threw it right to me. On the next play, we did the same thing again and scored.

Now he was smiling.

He said his yard shoes were slowing him up and he wanted to play barefooted. I said I wouldn't do that if I was him because there might be stickers, but he didn't care. Then he took off his old red shirt. Underneath, he was wearing one of those T-shirts that are cut out under the arms and have straps over the shoulders. There was a fresh tear in the back, plus lots of others.

"I'd throw that thing away if I was you," I told him.

"What thing?"

"That shirt's got so many holes. Why don't you wear another one?"

"Ain't got no other one. 'Cept for my going-to-church T-shirt."

"You wear a T-shirt to church?"

"Under my good shirt. One good shirt, one good T-shirt. Church only."

I concentrated real hard on setting the ball on the tee when he said that. I wasn't making fun of him. It's what I would have said to any of the guys—but they all have plenty of T-shirts.

The Rebels were a pass-completing machine. Dee kept sailing perfect spirals, and I kept hauling them in. I dropped one, and a tree intercepted one, but the rest of the time, we were unstoppable.

But Stokes is smart. Every time Dee had Andy covered, Stokes would keep it or dump it off to Calvin, and they would make five or six yards before I could get there, so they kept making first downs. Then when they got close to the goal line, Stokes handed off to Andy on an end around and he beat us over the goal line.

It must have been more exciting to watch than our usual games. It seemed like almost every car that drove by that afternoon slowed down when they went by. Mr. Bethune even parked his big white truck and watched us. It made me feel important.

I kept one eye on Dee the whole time to make sure nobody was mean to him. At first they ignored him. But when everybody saw how he could throw the ball, they started treating him like a regular player.

When it was Nighthawks 14, Rebels 14, Stokes leapt like somebody in a flying circus, intercepted Dee's pass, and cut into the end zone just out of my reach.

"Luck!" Dee shouted.

"You mean skill!" Stokes shouted.

But they were smiling.

Leave it to Andy to try and mess everything up.

Dee was leaning over, retying his shoes, and Andy walked by and mumbled something. Dee shot up straight: "What'd you say?" Andy looked back and shrugged like he didn't know what Dee was talking about.

I called the Rebels into a pre-kickoff huddle.

"What'd he say to you?" I asked Dee.

"It was nothin'."

"I want to know."

"Well, y'all white boys talk kind of funny, but it sounded like he called me a name."

I almost asked what name.

If Andy could get Dee rattled, it would be that much easier for the Nighthawks to win, and nobody wants to win more than Andy does.

"Don't let it bother you," I told Dee. "We'll get him back by mashing his team in the dirt."

"Yeah!" Kenny said.

We had good field position after the kickoff and scored quick on a long bomb from Dee to me. Stokes answered with a bomb to Andy and it was Nighthawks 28, Rebels 21.

On the next kickoff, darn if Calvin didn't boot it all the way to where I was standing on the driveway. I was thinking so hard about running, I forgot to make sure I caught the ball first. By the time I picked it up off the ground, Andy was on top of me, and we ended up with first down on our own five-yard line, worst field position of the day.

On our first three downs we gained zero yards because Andy and Stokes doubled up on me and made it impossible to catch a pass. They had four touchdowns and we had three, and if we didn't score on this drive, the game was pretty much over.

We stayed in the huddle so long, they started yelling at us, but I was making up a play and it took a while. I called it the Rebel Rouser. Kenny snapped the ball to me and tried to stay in front of Calvin. I pitched the ball to Dee and took off running. Dee took three steps back and pump-faked a long pass to me. By this time Calvin was charging hard at Dee, but right at the last second, Dee floated the ball over Calvin's head, right into Kenny's hands. And since Andy and Stokes were both covering me, Kenny took off down the other side of the field. Nobody ever expected Kenny to get the ball. All he had to do was not drop it before he crossed the goal line.

He dropped it. Ten yards from pay dirt.

When he turned around to get it, he accidentally kicked it all the way back to midfield. Calvin had it in his fingers when I swooped down and snatched it away from him.

I had to score. Now.

A long time ago, when I was eight, a bunch of us were playing King of the Mountain on a giant dirt mound where they were building a new house. These three older guys were shoving everybody off the mountain every time we got close to the top. I remember I was lying on my back at the bottom of the mountain and I was so mad I just started screaming at whatever was not letting me be big enough and strong enough to charge up that hill and beat those guys. *Aaaaahhh!* And all of a sudden it felt like some kind of monster got inside me, and I *was* big enough, twice as big as those older guys and ten times more dangerous, and nobody and nothing could stop me. I charged up that pile of dirt and slung every one of them off until I was all by myself, screaming down at them, daring them to try and climb back up. Nobody tried. They looked like I had broken some rule by winning the game.

When I saw the football in my hands and only Andy, the jerk who had insulted my friend, standing between me and the goal line, that monster got into me. I came at him like Frankenstein in a Corvette, and he knew he better get out of the way or die.

"Touchdown, Rebels!" I flung the ball in the air.

"It worked!" yelled Kenny, like the plan had been for him to drop the ball and kick it the wrong way.

We had to make this extra point and the game would be tied. This time Dee played center and snapped me the ball. I pretended to hand it off to him and he ran outside to the right and took Stokes and Andy with him, while I walked into the end zone. Kenny ran like he had the ball, which was not part of the plan, and when he got across the goal line, Calvin landed on top of him. We call it "getting Calvined." It hurts. We had to wait for Calvin to push himself off the ground before we could see Kenny again and know that he was all right.

Nighthawks 28, Rebels 28. The next touchdown would win the game, it was our turn to kick off, and we hadn't stopped them from scoring yet.

I got everybody into a huddle.

"Listen up, y'all. This is it."

"What's the plan?" asked Dee.

"No plan. I'm going to boom it all the way down to the other end of the yard and we just have to stop 'em."

"We can't," huffed Kenny, still catching his breath from being Calvined.

"This time we will," I said.

"We could call it a tie and do something else," Kenny said.

"No we couldn't."

"It's just a game," he said.

"No," I said, "it's not just a game."

He would have been right any other day. Winning isn't usually that big a deal. You cheer for your side, make fun of the other team, and get something to drink. But today we had to win because *Dee* had to win. Then nobody could say he didn't deserve to play with us.

Kenny made a fake whistle noise and raised his hand in the kickoff signal and brought it down. I ran to the ball.

I tried to kick it too hard, like I do everything too hard, and got my foot too far under it, and it hung in the air like a wounded duck, barely past midfield.

Calvin was watching it come down, waving his arms for a fair catch.

"You can't fair-catch a kickoff!" screamed Andy.

Calvin turned around to Andy and the ball bounced off his head right into Dee's hands. Dee streaked downfield and crashed into the end zone. Rebels 34, Nighthawks 28, Roses −5.

"Rebels win! Rebels win!" Kenny was spinning like a crazy person with his arms stretched out.

"Woo-hoo, mercy!" I yelled.

The Nighthawks were standing around looking at each other like they couldn't understand what had happened.

"No fair!" Calvin yelled.

"Once it goes ten yards, it's anybody's ball, remember?" Dee said.

"Yeah, but . . . he went too fast!" Calvin said.

Some of the roses were just bent and some were all the way torn off. I checked the house to see if Mama was watching and told Dee it was okay, that it had happened before. I hid the broken ones in the pine straw and propped up the others. Then I put my arm around his shoulder and held up the ball like a trophy.

Andy was so mad, he was almost crying.

"Dee can haul butt." Stokes was still panting. "I'll grant you that."

"Dee!" At first I thought Willie Jane was cheering along with us. "Dee! Come here right now!"

He ran to her. What could be wrong?

She pulled him in close. I only heard "Now get on back to work."

"What's going on?" I asked him when he walked back.

"My mama said you need to go see your mama, and I need to get back to work."

Mama was pouring iced tea into some glasses on a tray.

"Listen, Trip, Meemaw's dropping by to show me some fabric."

"Fabric?"

"Who knows, we might also talk about what kind of Halloween treats she's going to make this year." She looked at me with her eyebrows up and her lips tucked in, like I was supposed to get all excited about Halloween treats. "Now I need you to—"

"Mama, Dee just won the game for us! How come he has to start raking again?"

"It would be best if Dee did what he was hired to do. Your grandmother does not need to see him playing football with y'all."

"What would be so terrible?"

"What would be so terrible? Do you want to give her a heart attack? Now tell everybody to run along and go down to the Gibsons' and get Farish, will ya, honey?"

"This doesn't make any sense."

"It makes sense that I am asking you to do something, Trip Westbrook. Now hop to it!"

I did what I was told, but I kept thinking, Heart attack? Meemaw is old-fashioned, but she's nice. She and Papaw are always smiling at everybody. It would give her a *heart attack* to see Dee playing with us? She's the one who taught me that Jesus loves all the children of the world. "Red and yellow, black and white, they are precious in his sight." Meemaw used to sing me that song and read me Bible stories and rock in her rocker by me until I went to sleep, which wasn't easy with all that creaking.

One night she told me to listen carefully, that she had something real important to tell me. She said that when she was a young girl, not even married to Papaw yet, she caught special pneumonia and nobody thought she was even going to live much longer. Then, one night when she was lying in her hospital bed, Jesus came to her standing in a cloud, and she promised Jesus if he would let her live, she would go to church every chance she got. Jesus said all right, and she got well the next day. And it was a miracle.

That's why we went to church so much.

Meemaw is president of the WMU, which stands for Women's Missionary Union. One time at a party, I heard Daddy say it stood for Wild-Eyed Matrons United, and it wasn't the hooch that was gonna kill Papaw, it was that good old-time religion.

I went out and sat on the front porch. Dee was raking hard. I didn't know exactly what to say to him, since I didn't know how to explain that it was okay for him to play football with me and my friends but not if certain people were watching.

Finally I said, "Sorry you had to go back to work."

He shrugged. After playing on the same team with him, it shouldn't have been so hard to think of something to say. Then I said, "So how come your name is Dee? Is that short for something?"

"My mama said she named me after the movie *Demetrius and the Gladiators*. She saw it right before I was born."

"Why did she want to name you that?"

"Because none of the other gladiators could beat Demetrius. Couldn't anybody beat him. He killed three tigers with his bare hands. She said she wanted her little boy to be tough like that 'cause she knew I would have to fight for everything I got, like every colored boy."

"You sure play football like a gladiator. Has she ever seen you?"

"I don't guess so."

"Next time we'll tell her to watch."

He looked at me like he wasn't so sure about there being a next time.

"How come your name is Trip?"

"My daddy is Samuel Thompson Westbrook Junior, which makes me Samuel Thompson Westbrook the Third, so they call me Trip, like 'triple,' get it?"

"I get it."

"Mama is Virginia Lynn McKenna Westbrook and my sister Ginny Lynn is named after her. Meemaw's name is Farish McKenna and my sister Farish is named after her."

"Oh."

"But it's hard to think about Meemaw having any other name besides Meemaw, you know?"

"Ain't got a meemaw."

"You don't have a grandmother?"

"Or granddaddy either. Died before I was born. Don't even have a daddy anymore. He lives in St. Louis."

I didn't figure he wanted to talk about that, so I didn't ask anything.

Mama came out to the porch.

"Did you get all cleaned up? Hey, Dee." She smiled at him like "Isn't he cute?"—the way she smiles at a puppy.

Then she looked at the rose bed and the smile went away. She tromped down the steps and marched over to the rose bed and stood there with her hands on her hips. She reached out and tried to make the propped-up ones stand up by themselves, but they flopped over as soon as she let go. Then she dug around and picked up the ones I had hidden. I thought I buried them better than that.

"Trip Westbrook! Do you want to explain this?"

One hand was on her hip and one hand was full of broken roses. She was mad, mad, mad.

"What have I told you about getting into my roses?"

"Ma'am?"

"Don't you act like you don't know what I'm talking about."

"Well, I, uh—you mean *those* roses?"

"You are cruisin' for a bruisin', young man!"

"Miz Westbrook," said Dee. "It wasn't Trip that . . ."

I frowned at him and shook my head. When Mama's eyes get black like that, you do not want to be the reason. She was the kind of mad she gets when her day has been too busy with errands and projects and meetings, and she needed to lie down and take a nap a long time ago, but people would not let her take a nap and somebody, somebody was going to have to pay for this.

"He means we don't exactly know what happened, Mama. We don't exactly know who broke your roses. We tried to be so careful."

"And those you propped up, you might just as well have broken off. They're not going to make it. Do you exactly know who bent them and then propped them up like that so I wouldn't notice, instead of telling me honestly what had happened?"

"Well . . . well, I was gonna tell you about it as soon as you got home."

"Miz Westbrook, the truth is . . ." Dee still did not understand that he was in danger.

"The truth is that I did it, Mama. I couldn't stop running in time and ran in there and accidentally broke them and tried to hide it from you. I'm sorry."

She stared at me and you would not have thought that I was her beloved firstborn, you would have thought that I was a redheaded stranger and the punishment didn't exist that was horrible enough for me, but she would invent it.

Probably the biggest reason that I'm a good kid is that I'll do anything not to make Mama that mad. The last time I saw her like this was a few months ago, when I rode on the back of a motorcycle. Daddy always said he would buy me a car when I got to college if I promised never to ride on a motorcycle. Mama told me he had a friend in high school who got killed in a motorcycle wreck, and that's why he felt so strongly about it. He also said he would pay me a thousand dollars when I was twenty-one if I never touched a cigarette or a beer until then. That part sounds like an easy thousand. But I have always wanted to know what riding motorcycles felt like. Mama and Daddy left for a party one Saturday afternoon, and I was hanging out in the yard and here came Johnny Adcock on his new Yamaha YM1, which he was almost old enough to legally ride. He said he would take me around the block.

I would see what it felt like and never do it again. Just around the block. It wasn't like I was driving it myself. Anyway, who would ever find out? So I got on the back and hung on to Johnny, and we took off around the corner. He opened it up all the way down Waynedale, and I was so happy I had made this decision.

Then, soon as we turned back onto Oak Lane Drive, even though they weren't supposed to be home until late, here came Mama and Daddy. I ducked as low behind Johnny as I could, but it was too late. They were standing in the driveway, waiting for me. Mama had forgotten a cheese ball for the party. So thanks to that cheese ball, I got into the worst trouble I'd ever been in and finally understood what God was trying to tell me: *"You will never get away with anything."*

Now Mama turned before she went back inside and shook the dead roses at me: "When Meemaw leaves, you and I are going to improve your understanding of 'yard rules' and what happens to those who violate them."

The chances of me ever playing football in the front yard again didn't look very good. Or of ever being let out of my room again.

I decided to stay outside until Meemaw came. Dee went back to raking, and we talked about school. He has a lot more kids in his classes than I do, thirty-five or forty, and the teacher has to spend so much time making everybody act right, she hardly has any time left to teach anything. He said he didn't mind school, that he wanted to learn about stuff, especially arithmetic, which I personally cannot understand anybody wanting to learn about. He said he learned more from reading library books on his own than he did in class.

He asked me what seventh grade was like, and I told him I liked walking around on my own and having a lot of different teachers. But I was still getting used to how many more people there were at junior high. Plus, the PE classes are run by mean old guys with paddles. The meanest was the head football coach, Coach Montgomery, who had long teeth and a long nose. Stokes said it looked like a ski jump for flies. Coach Montgomery made us run laps until we collapsed on the track, and climb ropes with our bare hands until we had rope burns and couldn't hold on anymore.

When Coach Montgomery asked me why I didn't go out for football, and I told him about Mama wanting me to wait a year, he looked at another coach and laughed. He said, "Gotta wait till Mommy says it's okay? That boy doesn't want to play football." What he meant was "You are a sniveling little sissy who doesn't deserve to go to my school, and I am going to hurt you every chance I get."

It's bad enough the coaches make you run around for an hour and only give you ten minutes to take a shower and get dry before your next class, but if you mess up the slightest bit or even if they just think you're not trying hard enough, they'll make you grab your ankles and give you some licks with those paddles just for the fun of it. They drill holes in the wood to make it hurt more.

"I had never even had a man teacher before this year, much less a mean man teacher with a paddle," I said to Dee.

"Sounds pretty rough."

Meemaw pulled up in the driveway in her brand-new Cadillac. The late-afternoon sun lit up her earrings and her necklace and her big smile when she leaned down to give me a hug. She's sixty-something, but I can see why people say she's still beautiful.

"How is my big man doin' today? Just getting so taaalll . . ."

Even though I see her all the time, she likes to look surprised and say how I'm getting so tall, like tall is the best thing anybody could possibly be. I wish I really was getting so tall, like Daddy. He says be patient.

Meemaw walked up the steps slowly, watching her feet.

"That's Dee," I said, pointing.

"What, sweethaht?"

"Willie Jane's son."

"Well, hello, Dee," she said, laughing.

"This is Meemaw."

Dee held up his hand and smiled.

"Dee's a good raker," I told her.

"I can see that," said Meemaw. "Don't woik too hahd, Dee."

"He's a good football player, too," I said, but she was already opening the front door and singing "Woo-ooo" like she always does instead of knocking.

Farish and Ginny Lynn and me sat in the living room with Meemaw and had a "nice visit." We only have to sit there long enough to talk about something great we've done lately, and then we can go. Later, Mama called us back to the living room to say good-bye and Meemaw said, "Love ya good," and hugged us and drove off.

Mama declared that she was going to take a nap before supper. So that was good. She might be in a whole different mood by the time we improved my understanding of yard rules.

The kitchen smelled like fried chicken, which is probably the best smell in the world, and also like turnip greens, which are slimy and stinky. Why do people pretend turnip greens are okay to eat? Daddy says they're good for you and puts hot sauce on his.

Willie Jane put on her sweater and called Dee into the house to say good-bye.

"Tell ya mama when she's awake that everything's ready, she just has to warm up the rolls."

She picked up a sack of cantaloupes Mama had gotten for her at the farmers' market and said she would see us Monday.

Dee whispered, "Thanks for not telling your mama who tore up her roses."

"Oh, that's okay," I said. "You're too young to die."

Then he held out his hand. It seemed kind of like out of a movie, this kid shorter than me trying to shake hands like we were grown-ups. I just looked at him for a second. But he kept it out there, smiling at me. So we shook.

I was reading about the Trojan War, but my mind kept wandering to new plays for the game next weekend when me and Dee would beat 'em again. When I glanced up from my book, Daddy was standing in the doorway, which can be a scary surprise because he fills up the whole space. He played basketball at Tulane.

"Hi, pal."

Mama came up behind him and said they were wondering if we could "chat" for a minute. They came in and sat on the end of the bed. Here came the yard rules. I clenched my toes.

But they didn't seem mad. They seemed *sorry* about something. They hadn't said anything sad at supper. Maybe they wanted me to know before my sisters did. I had a sudden, terrible thought: Meemaw's dead!

"Your mother tells me that Dee played football with you and the gang yesterday."

What was sad about that?

"You oughta see him throw a pass, Daddy. He's real fast, too."

"Well, I think it's great that you included Willie Jane's boy in your game, but it's just that sometimes there are, well, larger issues involved, and—"

"We've gotten some phone calls," Mama said.

"About what?" I asked.

"There are concerns among the neighbors," said Daddy. "They are concerned that—"

"Listen, honey, this is all my fault," Mama said. "I told you it was okay for Dee to play with y'all, but . . . he really doesn't need to be out there in the front yard like that. It upsets people."

"What? He was playing football! He wasn't hurting anybody!"

"We know, pal," Daddy said.

"Well, what are people all concerned about? Who called, anyway?"

They just looked at me. Then Mama said, "Mrs. Sitwell, Mr. Bethune—"

"Mr. Bethune? Mr. Bethune parked his truck and watched us play! Why would he stop and watch us if he—"

"It doesn't matter who it was, Trip. They are our

neighbors and a whole bunch of people around here, not just Pete Bethune, but a *whole* bunch of people are upset about having to integrate schools—"

"And neighborhoods," said Mama.

"The Civil Rights Act," I said.

"Yes."

"Miss Hooper told us all about it in history."

"Then you can understand why people are upset."

"But I don't understand. I hear people at school saying bad stuff about colored people—they're lazy, you can't trust 'em—and I want to say, 'When did you ever hang out with colored people to know anything about them?' I wouldn't say those things about Willie Jane and Dee. Would you?"

"Of course not, honey," Mama said. "Your father and I—"

"So what would be so bad if some of the kids at school were colored?"

Daddy was thinking. Mama leaned over and put her hand on mine and smiled that smile that says "We both know how right I am."

"It's not that anything is wrong with colored people, honey," she said. "It's just that they are different. And we can't have them going to our schools and living in our neighborhoods, can we? When you're older, you'll understand."

I pulled my hand away. "I don't see why not." Maybe

I sounded kind of crazy, but it was said, so I looked hard at both of them. "I don't see what everybody's so worried about." I looked at Daddy. "Are *you* worried?"

He stretched his lips like it was something he didn't know how to talk about. "It's a complicated issue, pal. I see colored patients every day and listen to their problems. I know things need to change."

Daddy cares about his patients. They come up to me in the grocery store and say I must be Dr. Westbrook's son because I look just like him, and he delivered all their babies, and they love him so much. One lady told me how he saved her life and started crying right there in the cereal aisle.

"So do the colored ladies still have to sit in a different waiting room?" I asked.

"Don't be disrespectful," Mama said.

"I'm just asking."

Daddy took a deep breath. "I'm working on the waiting room issue. I have a couple of people on my side up there."

"But Dee playing ball with us is simple. You used to play ball with colored kids in New Orleans. That's all I was doing."

"That was a different time and place," Daddy said. "Look, your mother and I are not like these people who have been calling and complaining, and I would never want you to think we are."

"They're a bunch of mean, stupid people. Especially that old bag Mrs. Sitwell."

"Trip Westbrook!" Mama made a shocked face.

"I'm sorry."

"Some of them *are* stupid," Daddy said. "Or at least ignorant."

"And we're not giving in to them, right?" I said.

They looked at each other and didn't say anything. And it hit me: they had come in here to tell me something, and now they didn't agree on what to tell me. It felt strange. I knew they didn't always agree. Mama teased Daddy about being a "soft-hearted liberal." But when it comes to us kids, they're always together. One voice makes the rules around here, the Mama-Daddy voice.

Mama finally said, "Honey, we simply cannot allow—"

"No, pal," Daddy interrupted, "we are not giving in to them. Y'all go ahead and play with Dee. We just wanted you to know what was going on."

He stood up like that was all that needed to be said. Mama looked at him like she was definitely not finished. Then she walked out real fast, and Daddy went after her.

"That is not what we—" Mama whispered.

Daddy whispered something.

Then Mama said, "We have to live here, Sam!"

I heard Mama say at a party once that she said she was "bound and determined" to get out of Mississippi and go to college in New Orleans, which was where she fell in love with Daddy. And it was hard to bring home this "exotic" older man as her fiancé. I looked that word up, "exotic." It means "unusual."

It didn't matter to her parents that Daddy was almost a doctor; what mattered was that he was from the Marigny district of New Orleans, where a lot of poor people lived. They expected her to marry somebody from a rich family no farther away than the Delta. Daddy was just part of a rebellious phase, they said, which had started when she picked Sophie Newcomb over Ole Miss, where all the Jackson debutantes went.

It took forever to get their approval of her marriage, and she wasn't sure she had it yet. But if they ever cut her off, she said, she had her degree and would enjoy using it. It was hard to hear her say "my parents" and put that together with Meemaw and Papaw. I don't think I wanted to put it together.

Mama and Daddy were having one of their serious talks at the dinner table, and the rule when that happens is that children must temporarily lose their hearing. They started out on Martin Luther King and his marches and speeches. Daddy was all for him,

Mama was undecided. Then Daddy talked about when Governor Barnett tried to keep James Meredith from going to Ole Miss, and the military police came. "People died because a colored man wanted to go to school with white people," Daddy said, like he dared anybody to believe it.

Mama said she did not agree with Ross Barnett about everything, but some of her lifelong friends had been his strongest supporters, and the new reservoir was named after him, for goodness' sake. Daddy said Barnett was a buffoon. Mama cut her eyes at us to remind Daddy who else was at the table, even if we had temporarily lost our hearing.

But that made Daddy talk even louder about all kinds of stuff, like he would rather get his information from the national news on TV than from that racist rag of a newspaper we have here in Jackson, and he would cancel our subscription if Mama would let him; and if we expect Negro men to go fight in a war with white men, it's "high time they had the same chances in life when they got back"; and he's worn out from trying to get the other doctors at his OB-GYN clinic to open the waiting room to colored patients, instead of making them sit somewhere else, and the other doctors won't do it because they're a pack of self-interested, nearsighted racists.

Mama raised her eyebrows at Daddy and said, "Well, *I* am not a racist."

Daddy raised his eyebrows and didn't say anything. "I say 'colored person' or 'Negro,'" Mama said. "Never that other word that starts with n, or any other ugly term. Unlike a lot of people around here."

The other day when we were taking Willie Jane home because her Buick wouldn't start, Mama said she wanted me to go too, because Daddy was still working at the hospital and she wanted a man in the car. I felt good being the man in the car, but kind of bad that Willie Jane has been my other mama my whole life and I didn't have any idea where she lived. I never pictured her in any house but mine.

Farish and Ginny Lynn sat in the back with Willie Jane, and I sat up front with Mama. We drove way out on Woodrow Wilson Boulevard across a couple of bridges before we turned onto her street. She still lives in a shotgun shack, like the one she told me about living in when she was a girl, all crowded up with others just like it. The only fences are chicken wire, and the yards are either all dirt or all weeds. It's like even the trees don't want to be there. I knew colored people don't have as much as we do, but I guess I never knew how much they don't have.

I met Mama's eyes, and I knew we were both thinking how run-down and sad everything looked. Then Ginny Lynn piped up: "Uh-oh, we're in colored-town!"

I slunk down as far as I could go. Mama sat up and

looked like she was ready to yank some hair out of somebody's head.

"Where in the world did Ginny Lynn hear that name?" She was using her trying-to-be-calm voice, but her eyes had gone black.

"She didn't hear it from me!" Farish said.

"Me neither!" I said.

"Well, somebody taught it to her," Mama said. "Ginny Lynn, honey, we don't say that. Now tell Willie Jane you're sorry."

"I'm sorry," Ginny Lynn said.

"That's okay, sweet girl." Willie Jane laughed and tried to make Mama feel better, because who knows what a four-year-old white girl will say?

All the way back to our house, me and Farish had to convince Mama that we had never used that name in our lives and there were lots of other places Ginny Lynn could have picked it up besides from us. Mama admitted we were right, but her eyes were still black. When she says she's not a racist, she's telling the truth.

I didn't get up until after ten. Willie Jane was loading the dishwasher when I went into the kitchen.

"Mornin', Mr. Sleepyhead."

"Mornin'. Where is everybody?"

"Farish is down the street. Ginny Lynn's watching

cartoons. Ya mama runnin' errands and ya daddy is trying to rest. You missed the pancakes."

"Huh?"

"Buckwheats."

"Aw, come on, Willie Jane."

She knows buckwheats are my favorite.

"What you expect, you come in the kitchen so late? No more batter."

"You can make some more."

"Unh-unh, I got to vacuum. Ya mama want me to vacuum this whole house today. *And* finish the ironing *and*—"

"Ple-e-e-ease. . . ."

"Can't do it."

"Come o-o-o-o-n. . . ."

She closed up the dishwasher and turned it on and turned around.

"I can show *you* how to make 'em," she said.

"I don't feel like learning how to make 'em. I'm too sleepy."

"Then I guess you gonna have to ask yourself, 'Am I more hungry or am I more sleepy?'"

"I'm sleepy *and* hungry and you're the maid."

I wasn't trying to be mean, but dadgummit, I wanted some pancakes.

I knew she was mad, because she wouldn't say one more word. I kept sitting there and didn't say anything either. She got another big bowl out of the cabinet and started mixing up some more batter, and when she had made them, she kept on not saying anything and handed me my buckwheat pancakes.

I buttered them real good and poured molasses all over them and ate on the couch in the den so I could be away from Willie Jane.

Dee was working out front. If he would hurry up and finish the yard, we could do something till the guys got here for the game. Meanwhile, I couldn't find much of anything to do by myself. The last time I told Willie Jane I was bored, she had said, "Bored? On the best day of your life?"

"Why is this the best day of my life?" It was just a Tuesday.

"'Cause it's the one you have."

Now I find something to do.

I decided to finish my new Dracula model on the patio, where the paint fumes weren't so bad. The trick is to get that little speck of white in the eye. That's what makes them look alive. But even after I got my speck of white better than it's ever been, I had this feeling that making monster models wasn't as much fun as it used to be. I've been having that feeling a lot.

Mama took us to the fair last week. Everything smelled and tasted as good as ever. The midway was jam-packed with people, and the rides and games were all lit up as bright as ever. But the Ferris wheel seemed like the same old Ferris wheel, especially riding it with my sister, and even the Wild Mouse was something I had done enough times. Like I had used it up. The man running the Tilt-A-Whirl had a face like a leather map, and he was real skinny and missing teeth and did not seem to like anybody. I had never really noticed the people who run the rides.

I remember thinking when I was a kid that those paintings advertising Lobster Boy and Alligator Woman were the coolest part of the whole fair, and I couldn't wait to be old enough to go in there and have a look. But this year, Mama told me about those paintings, and she said they were probably just a man and a woman with fake scales and painted skin, or some poor unfortunates with birth defects, and how could anybody gawk at that? She said it was cruel. So now I don't want to go see them. I don't even know if I care about going back to the fair next year, which is something I thought I'd never say. I might just tell Farish to bring me some taffy.

She was out on the patio with me, playing with an old Hula-Hoop I found in the storeroom. Farish took one look and grabbed it and started spinning it around her waist. You won't catch me doing that.

I finished my Dracula and told Farish to put that Hula-Hoop down and throw me some passes. She said no. Because I wanted her to.

"You couldn't throw wet macaroni at a wall anyway," I told her.

The truth is, Farish has a good arm for a girl. She may be only eight, but she can handle a baseball pretty good. Mama says she's a tomboy and her new short hair suits her. Farish probably would have cut it as short as a boy's if Mama had let her.

"You couldn't throw applesauce at a balloon," she said.

"Twerp."

"Goob."

"Oooh, I'm gon' tell Mama you said 'goob,' " I said.

"No!"

There's nothing 'specially wrong with saying "goob," but Farish didn't know that.

"Throw me some passes or I'm tellin'." I handed her the ball.

She made a face like I smelled bad. "I'll throw from the patio. I do not feel like gettin' my feet dirty."

Farish *loves* to get dirty.

"Okay, you can stand on the patio and protect your precious tootsies."

"I'm gonna tell Mama you said 'tootsies.' "

"Let's see how you handle a football."

I was running a crossing route from one side of the yard to the other.

"All you have to do is get the ball to me when I come by," I told her. "Ready? On three."

She nodded and made her determined face. I got set.

"Hut one! Hut two! Hut three!"

Every time I got to where I was supposed to catch it, the ball hit the ground ten yards behind me and rolled down the hill. Superman couldn't have backed up fast enough.

After I ran down there and brought it back a few times, I said, "Farish, listen. Aim for in front of me."

"You mean throw it at the air?"

"Yes."

"If you say so."

I got into my stance.

"Hut one! Hut two! . . ."

Farish reared back and heaved it as hard as she could before I could even say "Hut three." It cleared the second flower bed and rolled on down to the creek.

"Farish!"

"I threw it at the air, Trip! That's what you said!"

"Here!" I handed her the Hula-Hoop and went after the ball.

The Hula-Hoop came wobbling by as I walked back up the yard.

"Look, I did it!" she yelled. "All the way to the creek!"

"And you're gonna have to go get it, too!"

She took off running and was almost to the spot when I remembered. I had been checking for that snake from a safe distance every day, feeling the same sick in my stomach, not wanting to ever see it again—but at the same time wanting to, so I could chop its head off and not have to think about it anymore.

"The snake! The snake! Farish! Don't move!"

"Where?" She bent over and started looking all around. I ran down and dragged her away.

"That's right where it was," I told her. "Still as a log. Just waiting for a dumb girl to put her foot on it."

"I want to see it."

"No you don't."

"Maybe it's over on the other side."

We stayed back from the bank and walked the length of the creek between our yard and Stokes's. It was hard to know for sure because the grass was so high in places, but we never saw it.

Then Farish said she wanted to get some sugar cane from Mr. Pinky's garden. I went back into the house to get a knife, and when I came out, Dee was on the patio telling Farish how glad he was to finally be finished with all that raking.

I invited him to come with us, and we walked down the backyard and over to the bridge and cut into Mr. Pinky's backyard. Mrs. Pinky was standing in her kitchen window, and I was afraid for her to see Dee with us. But she rapped on the glass and waved real big and smiled. At Dee, too. We stepped through the pumpkins, into the green jungle of sugar cane, and I sawed off a couple of joints of cane and stripped them and cut them into bite-size pieces.

We sat on the railroad ties between Mr. Pinky's garden and the Bethunes' yard and did us some chewin'.

There's nothing like sugar cane. It's like a chunk of fresh-cut tree that got soaked in water and grass and sugar. I warned Dee and Farish to be careful about running their fingers the wrong way on the ties. You don't want to get a splinter.

We chewed up our first batch and spit it out, and I cut some more. Farish was so busy chewing, she hardly said anything, which was a nice change. I showed Dee how I can squeeze my hands together and make fart noises come out from three different sides. He can do it with his armpit. Mostly we just sat and chewed. With some people I would have felt like it would be bad to let it get quiet. But with Dee, it didn't seem like we needed to talk unless we had something to say.

Mr. Pinky's back door slammed. His voice and a voice I didn't know were coming down to the garden. We could barely see them through the cane.

"Looks like your punkins are comin' right along," the other voice said.

Farish stood up, and I could tell she was about to yell "Hey, Mr. Pinky!" so I put my hand over her mouth and sat her back down. I don't know why. It wasn't like we were doing anything wrong. I just liked being hidden up in there.

"I tell you what, I ain't sleepin' too good since them trains started comin' through here so late," said the other voice. "That ol' bastud lays on that whistle."

"Ol' bastud."

Trains late at night don't bother me at all. They sound like news from the other side of the world.

"Punkins gon' be ready just in time for Halloween," Mr. Pinky said.

"Looks like it, looks like it."

"Y'all come get you one in a couple of weeks."

When they went back inside, Farish asked me, "What's an 'ol' bastud'?"

"Something bad," I told her. "And you're not supposed to say it."

I told Dee we oughta go get his mama to fix us some sandwiches because it was gonna be time to play football before too long. I bet him I could beat him back to the house, but he got there way ahead of me, which I already knew would happen. Farish got back to the house pretty fast too. For a girl.

Willie Jane was ironing and watching Ginny Lynn, and Dee begged her to let us change the channel to football. He said our TV was bigger than his.

We told Willie Jane we were starving and needed emergency sandwiches.

"Dee can have a sandwich," she said, "but you can't."

"What? Willie Jane, I'm sorry if I was mean about the pancakes, okay?"

"You still can't have a sandwich."

"Why not?"

"Ya mama say y'all are havin' a sit-down family lunch because she and ya daddy are throwin' a party tonight and there won't be time for a sit-down supper. A sandwich will spoil ya lunch."

"Oh, come on."

"She said heat up the leftover chicken and dumplings from last night, and cook some turnip greens to go with it and that's what you're gonna eat."

"I'm starving!"

"And y'all can't be messin' up in here either. Keep this house clean," she said. "Farish, play with ya sister while I fix some pimiento cheese."

"I will watch my sister," Farish said, "but I have absolutely no idea how to play with her, because she is four and I am eight."

She copies Mama all the time, like "I have absolutely no idea."

Willie Jane brought out a plate with three whole sandwiches after all, with potato chips, and milk with chocolate-flavored straws.

"Thanks, Willie Jane!" She knows how much I love her pimiento cheese.

The game on TV got boring and we started talking. Dee told me that the scariest show he ever saw was *Rodan*, about a giant bird monster. I told him about the picture of Moby-Dick in my *Book of Knowledge* collection. Moby-Dick is a giant white whale, big as a ship, and he's coming up out of the water with little beady eyes and a giant white jaw that would snap you in half. When I was little, it scared me so bad I'd drop the book. I still have to sneak up on that page.

I took Dee back to my room and showed him the Moby-Dick picture and my monster model collection. He said he wasn't scared of Moby-Dick, but he really liked my Frankenstein. He said he was gonna buy a Rodan model kit he could make. I'm pretty sure they don't make a Rodan model kit, but I didn't say that. There's no point in discouraging somebody unless you have to.

When Mama called everybody to the table, I asked her if Dee could sit with us.

"His mama told me Dee already had lunch."

"He could just sit with us."

"Dee can watch TV while we eat."

"But why can't he—"

"Because I said so."

Willie Jane brought out the chicken and dumplings with some corn bread and a big bowl full of turnip greens. Daddy asked her to please bring him some hot sauce for his greens and a glass of buttermilk to dip his corn bread in. I looked at Farish and we both made a face.

Daddy had just gotten up from a nap. He said he had to work until "the wee hours" last night. I love staying up until the wee hours. My main goal in life until I was seven was to stay up all night like Daddy.

It finally happened when Stokes's mom took us to see a movie that had a banshee in it. All night, me and Stokes looked out his bedroom window at the clouds sailing past a full moon, seeing banshees and leprechauns and all kinds of creatures. It got tough around four a.m., but we had made a blood-brother vow to stay up until sunrise and it felt great to have done it. But not as great as I wanted it to feel. And now I had to think of another main goal in life.

Daddy started talking about the clinic in Kansas City again and said he was gonna fly up there pretty soon to see if it might be a good idea for us to move there. Every time he brings up the idea of moving, the girls whine, and Mama and I look down and don't say anything.

"We're just talking about it, girls," Mama said. "It's nothing definite."

"Y'all can move if you want to," said Farish.

"Hush up and eat your turnip greens," Mama said.

"No thank you."

"Three bites. They're good for you."

"I can't even eat one bite."

"You heard me, young lady."

"Do as your mother says, Farish," Daddy said, like he really didn't care one way or the other.

Farish sighed and looked at her plate.

"Three bites," Mama said.

Farish put the smallest amount she could get away

with on her fork and nudged it into her mouth like Mama was making her eat cat spit.

"Turnip greens is for ol' bastuds," she said softly.

"What did you say, young lady?"

"I said turnip greens is ol' bastud food!"

Mama slapped Farish's hand, and Farish jumped up and ran to her room. Ginny Lynn's eyes got big as quarters.

Mama said, "Trip Westbrook, did you teach your sister that word?"

"No, ma'am."

"Well, who did? Did Dee teach it to her?"

"No, ma'am, Mr. Pinky said it. He didn't know we could hear him."

"You better not let me hear you sayin' it either."

"Yes, ma'am."

Then she shot a look at Daddy that said this was somehow all his fault. She said everybody was going to be here for the party in just a few hours, and she didn't know how she was gonna be ready in time.

We finished lunch quick. Mama jumped up and went into the kitchen and started giving more instructions to Willie Jane.

Daddy and I stayed at the table and talked about bad words. I asked him exactly what "bastud" means, and he said the word is *"b-a-s-t-a-r-d"* and it's somebody whose father isn't married to his mother. Then I asked him about "yay-ho," which is what Papaw calls people he doesn't like. Daddy said the real word is "yahoo," and it's from *Gulliver's Travels* by Jonathan Swift, and it means people who act like animals, not whoever disagrees with you, the way Papaw uses it.

Then I asked him if it was bad to call somebody a redneck. He said yes, because a redneck was an old-fashioned, uneducated person with old-fashioned, uneducated attitudes about most things, including colored people. He said he also knew some highly educated rednecks.

I told him Marcie Wofford called me a son of a bitch in the cafeteria when we were putting our trays up and I got banana pudding on her sleeve.

"What in the world is a seventh-grade girl doing using language like that?" he said.

"I don't know. I'm not a son of a bitch, though."

"Certainly not, son. Certainly not."

After lunch, me and Dee watched TV until the guys started showing up for the game. I promised Mama I would use all my allowance money for the next six months to buy her some new roses if we tore any up. I knew she did not agree with Daddy about letting this football game happen at all, and I knew it wasn't the roses she was really worried about. But she said okay.

I said I wanted Dee for my quarterback again, but

Andy said it wasn't fair to hog him, so this time Stokes and me and Calvin were the Rebels. Andy's team was the Viking Stompers.

Dee kidded Stokes that he'd better get ready to lose, and Stokes kidded him back. I guess I should have been glad that they were being friendly. But something bothered me about it. Dee was *my* idea. I was the one who discovered him.

Dee took off his red shirt and there was that same T-shirt that looked like it was about to come off in pieces. He took off his shoes, too, and said he couldn't even *feel* stickers, like he wanted everybody to know how tough he was. I liked it better last time, when he didn't seem so sure about everything. And he acted like he was just as happy to be on Andy's team as he had been on mine. Didn't he remember who called him a name last week?

Even more cars drove by this time, and most of them slowed down. Mrs. Sitwell came out to get her mail and stopped and watched us like we were criminals. I wanted to yell, "Go back in your house, old sourpuss face!"

The other reason I didn't want anybody watching was because the Rebels were getting stomped by the Stompers. The Dee-to-Andy pass combo was impossible to cover. Andy ran long almost every time, and Dee threw it just far enough ahead so Andy could reach out and pull it in without even slowing down. Nobody can defend against that.

Whenever I tried to catch a pass, Dee would bat it away and grin at me like I was supposed to say congratulations. He intercepted two.

The Rebels tried a couple of flea-flickers that would have worked against any other team, but the Stompers were always ready for it. Before things even got started good, the Rebels were behind 21–0.

"Y'all ready to give?" yelled Andy, being a terrible sport like always.

"It's five touchdowns to win," I told him. "Y'all have three."

"That's three more than y'all," yelled Dee, lining up for the kickoff. He was definitely feeling like one of the guys now, and I knew I should be glad, but the grin was really getting on my nerves.

Before Andy could kick it, I jabbed my fingers into the palm of my other hand in the time-out signal. "Time! Time!" I had an idea.

"What the heck?" yelled Kenny.

I huddled up with Stokes and Calvin.

"Look, y'all. A kickoff return might be our best chance. It's time to run the juggernaut."

They said "juggernaut" on *Combat!* the other night. That's one of mine and Daddy's favorite shows. I asked Daddy what "juggernaut" meant, and he said, "It means you can't stop it."

"Soon as I catch the ball, y'all come up on both sides of me and kind of cover me up and we all run together like a giant force that cannot be stopped."

"I can't run as fast as you," Calvin said.

"I won't be running that fast. It's not about speed, it's about power. Stokes is tall and you're wide and with both of y'all blocking them off as we go, they can't reach me. See what I'm sayin'?"

"I see." Stokes scrunched up his face like he didn't think it would work.

"We have to try *something*."

I stood way back because Andy had been booting it pretty good. When Kenny brought his arm down, Andy kicked a grounder that bounced into Calvin's hands.

I was yelling *"M-e-e-e-e-e-e!"* as hard as I could, but Calvin froze.

Just when Dee was about to tackle him, he turned around and pitched it to an invisible player between me and Stokes. I tore over there and snatched up the ball and yelled "Juggernaut!" and tried to twist away from Dee and fell.

"We're not playing tackle!" I said.

"It's not my fault!" he said. "Maybe that's why they call you Trip."

Everybody thought that was hilarious.

And then, before I could stop myself: "Maybe that's why they call you a . . ." I almost said it.

The way Dee looked at me . . . like he didn't trust me now. I turned out to be a typical white kid after all. I might as well have slugged him in the face.

"A what?" he said.

I tossed him the ball.

"A what?" he said again. I wanted to tell him he *could* trust me, but how could I say that in front of everybody? I walked back to the huddle.

"That jugger-thing didn't work," said Calvin.

"'Cause you didn't do it right, spazmo!" Stokes yelled.

"That's okay, that's okay," I told them. "We'll do it with a running play. Even better. Juggernaut on three."

Calvin snapped the ball to me and moved back to my right side and Stokes moved over on my left and we launched the juggernaut. We weren't even going Calvin speed, just slow, smooth, and steady. At first I thought we might go all the way. Then Calvin got tangled up with Andy, and Dee tried to get around Stokes on the left, and suddenly I was all by myself, so I took off. Kenny didn't catch me until I was ten yards into Viking Stomper territory.

"You can't cover up the runner like that!" Andy screamed.

"Yellow-bellied cheaters!" yelled Kenny.

The juggernaut had worked, just not the way I thought. So we did it again, and this time we scored.

We huddled up to figure out the extra point, and I got behind Calvin for the snap.

"Hut one! Hut two! Hut three!"

Calvin snapped the ball and pulled back to my right, Stokes shifted to my left, and we plowed straight over the goal line. It was perfect.

Somebody was yelling behind us.

"Hey, nigger!"

3

I could see Tim Bethune's ugly grin when I heard it. I didn't even have to turn around.

"You havin' fun, Sambo?" he said.

The scraping sound was his brother, Tom, dragging a baseball bat on the concrete. He was bunched up with Tim and Johnny Adcock and a couple of older guys. They were coming down the sidewalk like a pack of wolves.

I was thinking, Please keep walking, please keep walking, but they stopped and stood at the edge of the yard and looked at us the same way Coach Montgomery looks when he's about to use his paddle on you. I couldn't believe these were the same guys who used to play football and hide-and-seek with us. I wanted to say, "Hey Tim, don't you remember that time you showed me how to put cards on my bicycle spokes?"

Johnny Adcock used to play with us, too, until he decided he was a Beatle and started combing his hair all down in his face and wearing black all the time. They were all wearing boots and leather and black, and it was like they never knew us at all. What happens when you get to be a teenager?

"I said, are you havin' fun?" Tim stared at Dee.

Dee stared back.

"My brother asked you a question," Tom said, tapping his bat in his hand.

Calvin and Kenny looked like they were about to throw up. Even Andy looked scared.

"Well, I sure hope y'all have enjoyed your game," Tim said. "'Cause it's over now." Tom raised his bat and pointed to Dee with it.

"I don't know how that team can even see to play, with it being so dark over there." They laughed.

We got closer together, and I said to Dee, out of the corner of my mouth, "You ought to get in the house." He acted like he didn't hear me. Calvin and Kenny said they had had enough football for one day.

Then Stokes said, "Yeah, they only needed one more touchdown. They were gonna win anyway. Let's go."

Stokes and Andy walked off slow enough to show they weren't scared, but I knew they were. Kenny and Calvin ran behind the house. Me and Dee moved toward it. When we got to the porch, Tom yelled, "And don't let me see you out here again, colored boy! I'll bring this bat down on your head!"

We watched out the front window until they finally went on down the street. I felt so ashamed that I had let those guys talk to Dee like that, and boss us around and make us go inside. My cheeks were burning.

All I could do at first was look at the carpet. "Dee, I'm really sorry."

"That's okay."

"It's not okay. But there were too many of them," I said. "It wouldn't have been a fair fight."

"I guess not."

"I'm . . . I'm sorry about the other thing, too," I said.

He shrugged. I didn't know if that meant "Don't worry about it" or "I expected it to happen, white boy."

We went to the kitchen to get some apple juice. Willie Jane turned off the vacuum cleaner in the den and said she was finally through with this day. I didn't want to tell her what had happened to our game. Dee didn't say anything. But what if he told her later? All of a sudden I got this terrible feeling Dee might not be coming over anymore.

"Can he come back next Saturday, Willie Jane? Please?" I looked at him. "Don't you want to, Dee?"

"Sure." But he wasn't acting sure.

"You better think of a chore, if you want Dee to come back," Willie Jane said.

"What chore? The grass has about quit growing and the leaves are raked up good for a while. Why does he have to have a chore?"

"Ask your mama can she find somethin' else for him," she said.

"Okay, I'll ask. Y'all don't leave yet."

"Uh-uh, we gotta go. Don't bother ya mama, she's getting ready for her party. You have all next week to ask her."

"Please!"

I yelled through the bathroom door that I wanted Dee to come back next Saturday and did he have to have a chore, or could he just come over? Mama sloshed around in her tub and said it would be better if we had something for him to do. I heard them leaving the house.

"What can he do, Mama? Hurry!"

"Let me think about it and we'll tell Willie Jane on Monday."

"I have to know now."

"Why?"

"Because! Please, there must be something."

They were getting into the car.

"Well, we do need to get the flower beds ready for winter. I guess he could mulch."

I ran outside, and they were already driving off. I tore down the middle of the street, waving my arms and screaming, "You can mulch! You can mulch!"

They stopped. Dee rolled down the window and slid halfway out.

"What?"

"You can mulch in the flower beds!"

"What's that?"

"I don't know! But you can do it!"

He nodded and slid back into the car and they drove away.

I went back to my room and lay down. The more I thought about what had happened today, the madder I got. If only I had fought back. But I had chickened out.

I couldn't wait until next Saturday. If Tom Bethune came around scraping his bat, I'd take it away from him and bring it down on *his* head. Then I'd get Tim Bethune in a scissors hold so powerful it would squeeze his stomach in half. I'd light into those redneck jerks so hard, they'd beg me to stop. They'd be sorry they ever came into my yard. I would not chicken out again. I asked God to help me be brave and forgive me for almost calling Dee that word.

I keep my transistor radio on WRBC Rebel Radio Top 40. They play the best stuff. I put the radio under my pillow every night and it helps me fall asleep— unless they play a Beatles song. I'll stay awake for that.

They finally showed *A Hard Day's Night* in Jackson. It's not so much a good movie as a completely different movie from any I've ever seen. For one thing, I couldn't understand half of what those guys were saying.

The music was definitely the best part, but every girl in the theater was trying to scream louder than the girls in the movie. A little blond girl was crying in the lobby and screaming, "Good-bye, Ringo! I love you!" I looked at her for just a second and she kicked me and told me to shut up. I hadn't even said anything.

I told Mama I wanted to grow my hair long like the Beatles, and she said that was definitely not going to happen. I don't get why hair has to be such a big deal. The police are stopping people's cars if they have long hair. Some of the restaurants around here won't even let you sit down at a table if you have long hair. It's like you walked in with a sign: COMMUNIST ON DRUGS.

My all-time favorite way to fall asleep, though, is not listening to the radio. It's when Mama and Daddy have a party like they had last night. I lay there in the dark and listened and couldn't make out exactly what anybody was saying because my door was shut, but the sound of all that music and talking and laughing felt like a warm blanket to pull under my chin. I even like the smell of the cigarettes.

I was almost asleep when I heard Daddy and Dr. Freeman and Dr. Reeves talking in the hall. I've known Dr. Freeman since we moved from New Orleans to Jackson so Daddy could join his clinic. Dr. Reeves lives on our street. He's an eye doctor.

I could hear the ice tinkling in their glasses. Daddy was talking louder than usual and his words sounded blurry, which means he was drinking *liquor*.

I asked him about liquor one time, because Stokes told me liquor is illegal and anybody who drinks it is breaking Mississippi law. He said his dad has a bootlegger from Rankin County who leaves it in a sack at their back door. I told Daddy I didn't see how liquor could be illegal when him and Mama and everybody who comes to their parties drinks it. I've seen the bottles sitting out. They usually keep them locked up in a cabinet.

Daddy said he wasn't going to lie to me, that yes, anybody drinking liquor was "technically" breaking Mississippi law.

"Worse than that," he said, "they're breaking *Baptist* law."

Those are two kinds of laws I thought nobody was ever supposed to break, but Daddy kind of winked when he said "Baptist." And now he was out there with his glass, breaking the law again.

He was saying, real loud, "But why? Why have 'em wait in separate rooms?"

Dr. Freeman said, "Because that's how we've always handled it, Sam. You can't suddenly say, 'Hey everybody, coloreds and whites are gonna all sit together now!' What's the point of messing with the way things have always been?"

Then I heard Dr. Reeves say, "Sam's right. So far the HEW is only worried about hospitals, but they'll get to doctors' offices sooner or later, you know they will. Things can't stay the way they've always been. We have to obey the law."

"What the HEW wants and what will actually work in the state of Mississippi are two different things," Dr. Freeman said. "This new law wants the coloreds going to the same bathrooms, drinking at the same water fountains, going to the same schools, but do you see any of that happening? And it's not gonna happen."

"Sooner or later it will," Dr. Reeves said. "If Johnson has to bring in troops to enforce the Civil Rights Act, he'll do it. Just like Kennedy did at Ole Miss."

"Okay," said Dr. Freeman, "let's put 'em all in the same waiting room. What do you think that'll get us? I'll tell ya what. Delivery rooms full of mulatto babies! Is that what you want this country to look like in fifty years? Is that who you want running things?"

"I'm just sayin' it doesn't seem right," Daddy said.

"Has somebody been complaining to you about it?"

"No."

"Well, let's wait till they do before we get all hopped up on what's right for the coloreds."

"Somebody will be complaining, all right," said a voice I didn't recognize. "Martin Luther Coon is tellin' them they're all African kings and queens."

Daddy said, "I don't think that's what Dr. King wants to—"

"He just wants them to take over the country, is all," interrupted the voice. "With him as the grand poobah. He knows that every time he goes somewhere and gives a speech and stirs everybody up and has another march, more people are gonna get hurt and go to jail, the people he supposedly cares about. I'll tell ya who Dr. King cares about and that's Dr. King."

"Martin Luther King wants—"

"He wants 'em all to be up in white people's business. You mark my words. First it's waiting rooms, then it's restaurants, and before you know it, they're sitting next to you on the pew on Sunday."

"Now that's where I draw the line," said Dr. Freeman.

"Amen, brother," said the voice.

"Look, I just want what's fair for everybody," Daddy said.

Then his voice mixed in with all the others, and I didn't hear him again. I hope he said more about what's fair. I bet he did.

. . .

The first thing I saw when I opened my eyes was my clock, so I know the bomb went off at 1:37. It sounded like thunder right next to my head.

The party was over, and the house was dark. Farish was already out on the patio, holding Mama's hand. Daddy stood there with his arms folded. Everybody was coughing. The backyard was thick with smoke like the foggin' machine had just driven through. It smelled terrible.

"Dadgum bunch of idiots," Daddy was saying. Then he saw me and said, "It's all right, pal."

When the smoke cleared, we could see the hole in the yard.

"You think it was cherry bombs, Daddy?" I asked.

"It was more than cherry bombs."

Mama was madder than I've ever seen her. She was trying not to scream. "Call the police, Sam."

"What good would that do?" said Daddy. "We don't know who did it."

"Of course we know who did it!"

She meant the Bethunes.

Daddy told me everything was going to be all right and not to worry and to get on back to bed.

"It was the Bethunes," I said, since neither one of

them would say it. "Tim and Tom and some other guys saw us playing football with Dee yesterday." I almost said they came up in the yard and called Dee names and broke up our game. But then I would have had to say that I didn't fight back.

When I woke up, everything felt different. We had our usual Sunday breakfast, orange juice with banana slices in it and cinnamon rolls, but Mama was real quiet and it was hard to sit at the table.

I was still getting dressed when Daddy called me into their bedroom.

"Trip, your mama and I have been talking it over, and after what happened last night, we are going to have to say Dee can't play football with y'all after all."

"But you said—"

"He can still come over here, and y'all can play in the backyard all you want. Just not the front. Not till things calm down."

I didn't say anything.

"Okay, pal?"

I couldn't make myself say "okay."

"Okay?" Daddy said, like I better say something quick.

"Yessir."

I stood there some more. Mama came out of the bathroom in her robe.

"I know you're disappointed," Daddy said.

"Is everything going to be all right with the neighbors now?" I asked him.

"Of course it is."

"Everything is going to be just fine." Mama's eyes flashed like she would see to it.

"The Bethunes are bad people, aren't they?" I said.

"You don't want to talk about people being *bad*, Trip," Mama said.

"Mr. Bethune may have some bad *attitudes*," Daddy said to me, but he was looking at Mama.

"He provides for his family," Mama said. "They keep their yard nice. Remember when he helped us fix that flat tire? They go to our church, for heaven's sake."

"So they're good people?"

"Well, yes."

"Then why did they throw that bomb in our yard?"

"Trip, we don't know who—"

"But you said—"

"I think we were all a little overexcited last night."

So people can throw bombs in other peoples' yards and still be good. As long as they keep their yards nice and go to church.

I told Mama what Papaw told me about doing our Christian duty for colored people and that she ought to buy Dee some T-shirts because he had only two and one of them is all torn up. She didn't act like she was paying much attention when I told her that, but that night she came into my room and told me she wanted to go through my closet.

She pulled out a bunch of shirts and pants hanging in the back and took out a whole shelf full of sweaters and sweatshirts. She piled everything on the bed and went through it all, asking which ones I never wore anymore. I don't care about clothes that much in the first place, and I told her she could take it all if she'd let me go watch TV. She said she was giving my old clothes to Dee and he would grow into them. So then I wanted to stay.

After we'd gone through everything, Mama asked me if there was a coat I didn't wear anymore. My good old navy-blue coat—Mama calls it a pea coat—was so tight it was hard to move my arms. I said Dee could have that, too.

Next morning, Mama showed me two packages of T-shirts, six each, and said she was giving those to Willie Jane, too. I said I wanted to hand them to Dee myself, but she said it would be better if his mama did it. Then she said that just for my information, she was giving Willie Jane a raise, so I could quit worrying about that, too. I asked her how much of a raise, and she said that was none of my beeswax and to help her carry everything out to the playroom.

When Mama told Willie Jane all those clothes were for Dee, she set down her iron and hugged her.

"And look, Willie Jane." I held up the T-shirts. "Now he's got church T-shirts and school T-shirts, and plenty left over for football."

Then she hugged me.

She went through the pile, holding up each sweater and shirt and pair of pants. "So nice, so nice," she kept saying.

"He'll have to grow into these, but some of it might fit him now," Mama said.

"They'll fit him, they'll fit him," Willie Jane said.

She kept holding up the coat and looking at it.

I was hoping the Bethunes would forget about me and bother somebody else. It wasn't hard to stay away from them at school; the halls are crowded between classes, and ninth-grade lockers are nowhere near seventh-grade lockers. But it's different after lunch, when everybody goes outside and the teachers aren't watching. I can't get used to how much they aren't watching.

For six years we marched in single-file lines and everybody did everything at the same time. All of a sudden, nobody cares where we are as long as we make it to class. I could walk to the end of the hall in a crowd and keep on walking right out the back door. If I did it at the beginning of morning break, I could get a fifteen-minute head start before anybody knew I was gone. I kind of don't like knowing that.

Today in history class, Miss Hooper sent the boys out of the room for five minutes so she could say something to the girls. Marcie Wofford told me Miss Hooper told them to watch the way they sit. Skirts are definitely shorter than last year. You can't help but notice. Plus, it's like all the girls got together over the summer and said, "Okay, everybody, time for boobs!" I just want to know what they feel like.

Choral music is after history and then PE, which is right before lunch, which works out well since torture makes me hungry. They've been giving us all these physical fitness tests like how high can you climb a rope and how many chin-ups can you do—my answer is "not that high" and "one on a good day," no matter how many times they make me do it. I was getting some shorts from my locker when somebody tried to shove me in there.

"It's Dipwad Westbrook!"

Tim and Tom Bethune and a couple of ninth-grade football players were standing on top of me.

"Hey, *Dip*," Tim said.

"Yeah, *Dip*, yeah, *Dip*," they all said.

The bell for the next class was going to ring any minute, but I was pretty scared. I didn't let them see it. There was nothing I could say that would have made them leave me alone except that they were right and I was wrong. I stared right back at them and kept staring.

Then I thought of something to say. I said it real loud, too, in case any teachers were around who could get me out of this.

"Hey, Tim, when did you turn into this other guy?"

"What? Shut up."

"Remember when you used to hang around with me and Stokes and everybody? And you took me over to your house to show me your battleship models?"

"I said shut up."

"I mean, sure, you were a jerk in those days, too, but when did you turn into this other guy?"

"When you turned into a dip." He shoved me extra hard. "That's when."

I was trying to think of the next thing I would say when the bell rang, and they walked off.

"Watch it, punk," Tom said over his shoulder.

I was a little shaky in choral music. At least I hadn't chickened out.

But I was going to have to shove back next time, or get the snot beaten out of me.

I was still asleep when Willie Jane came banging into my room with the vacuum cleaner and roaring it all over the carpet. My clock said 7:49. On a Saturday morning.

"I know you're not asleep, I know you're not asleep," she kept saying. "You're the only one still in bed."

"I bet the girls are still in bed."

"Uh-uh. And your mama's about to be out of the house, and your daddy's playing golf. You need to get up and see Dee."

"Let me get dressed then," I told her.

Dee was sitting on the couch in his red shirt with his head sagging on his chest. He didn't seem real happy about being there. I hadn't seen him grumpy before. His eyes were usually wide open like they were trying to see whatever was next, but today they just wanted to be closed.

"I had to get up at six-thirty on a Saturday morning so I could get ready to come over here." His voice was small. "I didn't even get nothin' for my breakfast."

"I hate havin' to get up on Saturday."

"Reckon I could lie down somewhere? My stomach don't want to stay awake if it has to be this hungry."

"You can lie down in my room."

He closed his eyes, and looked like he might go to sleep any second.

"Or we could get something to eat," I said.

"Hmm," he grunted.

"What do you like for breakfast?"

"Pancakes."

"Yeah. Pancakes. Let's get Willie Jane, I mean your mama, to make us some." I was starving, too.

"I can make 'em," Dee said.

"What?"

"Mama taught me," he said. "She says I could go into the pancake business."

"Buckwheat pancakes?"

"Watch me."

I got up on a chair and pulled the special box off a high shelf in the pantry. Dee said to get eggs, milk, and butter. Dee put the skillet on the stove and said he needed some Wesson oil. I didn't know what he meant till he pointed to it. He put oil on a paper towel and rubbed it all over the skillet and turned the heat on. Medium high.

"Now we need a big bowl," he said. "And a big spoon, so we can stir up the mix with the milk and the eggs."

He cracked open the eggs and dropped them inside the bowl, but long strings of clear stuff dripped out of the shells and got all over the counter.

"It's hard to deal with eggs sometimes," he said.

"Sure is." I cleaned it up.

"Mama says don't stir it too much," he said. "Just till there aren't any big lumps."

When he had mixed it, he stuck his hand under the faucet and flicked water in the skillet.

"The water's not dancing yet. The way you know it's hot enough is when the water dances."

We waited a minute and Dee flicked water into the skillet again. It sizzled a little.

"Let's go," I said.

"Not yet," Dee said. "It's not dancing yet."

"Aw, come on." I never wanted pancakes so bad in my life.

"Not yet."

We waited some more, and the next time Dee flicked it, that water danced all over the skillet.

He spooned the batter into the skillet in circles that spread out.

"Wait till the tops bubble and the edges look hard before you flip 'em. If you wait too long, they get rubbery and dry. I like mine nice and soft. You want to flip 'em? Flippin' is the best part."

We watched until the tops of the cakes bubbled and the edges got hard.

"You gotta be careful." He handed me the spatula.

I did all right. Then all we had to do was watch them rise and take them off.

Dee put butter on them and put a paper towel on top so they would stay warm while we made the other three. He poured and I flipped.

I got us a couple of plates and forks. Now came the part where I could be an expert.

"What you want on 'em?" I asked him.

"Butter and syrup."

"Here's the important question—what *kind* of syrup?"

"What kind do *you* want?"

"Well, if you ask me, nothin' tastes better on a pancake than molasses. Farish puts maple syrup on hers. I call that Yankee syrup."

"I don't want maple syrup," said Dee.

"Heck no."

I got down the molasses and we sat at the kitchen table and went to town. Then we made three more apiece.

"What in the world are you boys up to in here?"

Willie Jane set down the vacuum cleaner and looked around the kitchen like a miracle out of the Bible had just happened.

"We made pancakes," said Dee.

"You want us to make you some?" I asked her. "There's plenty of batter left. Sit down and let us make you some."

"Child, I don't have time to eat pancakes."

"Dee said y'all didn't have breakfast this morning. Come on and sit down."

"Eat some pancakes, Mama."

She eased down at the table and watched us with a big, soft smile while Dee reheated the skillet and I restirred the batter and he spooned them in and I flipped.

"You want molasses, don't you?" I asked her.

"Goodness, yes, let me have some molasses."

Dee handed her the plate full of steaming pancakes. She took a bite and looked like she was thinking about it. Then she looked at us and said, "I tell you what, these may be the butteriest, sweetest, tenderest, best pancakes I have ever tasted."

Dee grabbed my hand and raised it with his like we had both won a boxing match.

"Winners and still champions!" he said.

"The Pancake Brothers!" I said.

Willie Jane said now that he had something in his stomach, it was time for Dee to do his chore. She took him out to the shed and showed him the mulch and the trowel and showed him what my mama wanted him to do. She said it wouldn't take nearly as long as mowing and raking. I said I would help him so we could get it over with, but she said Dee was getting paid for this job and he oughta do it himself.

I was kind of sleepy, so I went back to my room and lay down. The next thing I knew, Willie Jane was waking me up and telling me that Dee was almost finished.

Stokes was visiting his cousins in Bay St. Louis, and Andy had told me he had to do something on Saturday. I asked him what, and he said *"Something!"* like it wasn't any of my business. Calvin said he had something to do, too. So we couldn't have had a game today anyway.

Mama reminded me to keep Dee out of the front yard, but when I asked her how I was supposed to explain it to him, she said, "You'll think of a way." So I just didn't mention it. How do you say to a person, "My neighbors hate you so much, they told my parents not to let you play football with us anymore and even threw a bomb in our yard"?

Now, whenever I saw a neighbor, I wondered if they had called about Dee.

When Dee finished his mulching chore, I told him the guys couldn't come over today, and we oughta go in the backyard and see if that snake was still down by the creek. I told him I really wanted to see it again, which was sort of a lie and sort of not. He said he hoped we didn't see it, because he hated snakes, but he wasn't afraid to go down there. We walked the whole length of the creek on my side and then on Mr. Pinky's side and didn't see anything but a school of minnows. After a while the pancakes wore off, and we started getting hungry. Then I had an idea.

Papaw had told me that if I found an upstanding Negro who was hungry and wanted to eat in the Golliwog, he would buy him lunch. I didn't know where Papaw was more likely to be on a Saturday afternoon than the country club.

"I know where we can get some real good food," I told Dee.

I thought it was better not to tell him exactly where we were going. I just said we could ride our bikes there and it would be fun. He wanted to go into the kitchen and ask his mama to fix him a ham sandwich first. I told him that would defeat the whole purpose of the trip. He said he'd go if it wasn't too far, but he was hungry.

Mama and Daddy weren't home, which was a good thing, because they would have told me I was pushing too hard at everybody's limits, like I do. I could explain it to them later; I just had to get past Willie Jane. I told her we wanted to ride bikes and we would stay on the right side of the road with the traffic and use hand signals and be very careful, and we wouldn't be gone long—which was all true, depending on how long "long" is. She was loading the washing machine and said, "Okay, but hurry back."

I hadn't ever ridden my bike all the way to the club before, but all we had to do was pedal up to Old Canton, take a left, and keep going. It wasn't until we got out to the shed that I remembered there were only two bikes and one of them was Farish's. It was small and pinkish with pink and red and white plastic streamers coming out of both ends of the handlebar. I didn't know what else to do but play Rock, Paper, Scissors. Dee won, and I called for best two out of three. Dee won again, and I had to rethink the whole plan.

What if some of the guys saw me riding this thing? What if Coach Montgomery saw? He'd find a reason to paddle me every day from here to June. Did I want this bad enough to be pinky boy with streamers all the way down Old Canton Road? I almost told Dee we oughta forget the whole thing. Then I thought about all those mean people who called up and complained about us playing football together and I hopped on Farish's bike.

We had to ride single file on the edge of the street and sometimes in the dirt along the edge. A couple of cars blew their horns at us. One guy yelled, "Get off the road!" I think it was about us slowing down traffic more than anything, but I bet they were wondering what a white kid and a colored kid were doing riding bikes together. When we got to Shipley Do-Nuts, Dee wanted to rest for a minute in the parking lot.

"You said it wasn't that far," he said. "I'm starvin'."

"We're more than halfway there," I told him, hoping that was true. "It would take longer to go back than it would to keep going, and we wouldn't have gotten any food."

"We can get a donut right here."

"You got some money to get a donut?"

"I ain't got no money."

"Me neither. Where I'm taking you, we don't need

any money. We can eat all we want and I just have to sign a ticket."

"What kind of a restaurant doesn't take money?"

"It's not a restaurant, it's a club."

"What kind of club?"

"The kind that has the best cheeseburgers in town. Come on."

We rode past the shopping center and the big church and blocks of houses with shingles that all look alike and then it was fields and we started going uphill. I knew we were getting close. After a while, my lungs were burning like they do on the last lap in gym class when it would feel so good to stop. But I never do stop, no matter how much it hurts. If I'm going to play split end next year, I have to show Coach I can run all day. I'd rather be last than stop. But it was a lot of uphill, and I had to stand up on the bike to keep going. I looked back at Dee and he was standing up, too.

"We're almost there!" I shouted over the cars. I was breathing so hard it was hard to talk at all. "It's . . . gonna be up on the right."

"Well, it needs to hurry up and be there," shouted Dee.

Finally, there it was, the big country club sign. We had to lay our bikes down and rest. My legs were killing me, but what hurt worse was how wrong I had been about this ride being easy. It had been too far, too full of cars, too uphill. How could the real ride turn out so different from the one in my head? I knew I should tell Dee I was sorry for being that wrong, but I could barely admit it to myself.

Luckily, the road that curves around to the main entrance was all downhill. We took the left side of the entrance drive and leaned our bikes against the front of the Teen Wing. I walked Dee to the main entrance. He was looking around at the marble sidewalks, picture windows, fountains, and flowers.

"Looks like some kind of king lives here," he said. "I can't go in this place."

"Why not?"

"You know why not."

I knew, all right. But I pretended I didn't, because I wanted to prove that nothing terrible would happen and every redneck who didn't like it could go jump in a water hazard. If I could find Papaw, everything would be all right.

"You *are* hungry, aren't you?"

"I'm starvin'."

"Well, my family belongs to this club, my papaw was one of the people who started it, and I say you can go in there."

He still didn't want to.

"Dee, we rode all this way. You know you want a cheeseburger."

He shook his head and shrugged his shoulders.

I pushed open the big door and pulled him in after

me. We walked down the long entrance hall into the giant lobby, and there were a bunch of ladies playing cards. Everything was loud and flowery. A sign said it was a bridge tournament. They looked up one at a time and stopped talking and kept looking.

I waved to Mama's friend Mrs. Weatherly and smiled and said "Hey." She made a face like her chair was uncomfortable and kind of raised her hand, but it must have been too heavy for her to wave it. I was hoping some of those ladies were the ones who had called Mama and complained about Dee. "Take a look at how much I care what you think!"—that's what I wanted to say to all of them.

Their voices started up behind us when we cut down the stairs: "What in the world is Trip Westbrook doin', walkin' around in the lobby with that boy?" "Is he the child of somebody who works here?" "Unacceptable." "I'm going to call Virginia the minute I get home."

Kids' voices were pouring out of the Golliwog into the hall. I told Dee to wait there while I checked around for Papaw.

"Trip, I don't need to be standing here by myself. You heard those women. We need to get outta here." He looked pretty nervous.

I told him I would be right back and not to worry. Papaw wasn't in the locker room, so I stuck my head into the 19th Hole. I didn't really expect to see him there because they serve liquor. He was probably out on the golf course.

I told Dee to wait just one more second while I went into the Golliwog to see what was going on. A bunch of little kids wearing cone hats were jumping around, laughing and hollering, blowing noisemakers. There was a three-layer chocolate cake I could smell from the door on the center table and a giant HAPPY BIRTH-DAY sign strung across the ceiling. I didn't know any of the moms, but I'd seen them around. They were screaming louder than the kids, trying to get them to calm down because it was time for cake and ice cream. The Dentons were having lunch by the picture window.

Shelby came out with a tray full of ice cream and started setting bowls down for all the kids. I was glad to see him. He would take care of us.

"Hey, Shelby!"

"Hey there, Mr. Trip."

"Looks like they got you pretty busy today."

"Lord, yes."

He was too busy to stop, so I walked with him as far as the door the waiters come out of.

"Y'all aren't closed for this birthday party, are ya?"

"We open."

"So I can get a cheeseburger?"

"Go sit down over there, I'll be over directly."

"Can my friend have one, too?"

Shelby smiled and frowned at the same time, like he didn't know why I would ask such a question.

"Course he can!"

They were singing "Happy Birthday" when I pulled Dee into the room. Their voices kind of trailed off when we walked in and sat down. The mom at the table next to us made everybody get up and herded them to the other side of the room. She looked over her shoulder at us like we had a contagious rash. The Dentons got up and left. I didn't care. Shelby would be on our side. He would be glad to see a colored boy eating in the Golliwog for a change. I might ask him to join us when he was through working.

It was a lot quieter now. The little kids looked at us a second and went back to their cake. But the moms kept looking and whispering to each other.

"This isn't such a good idea," Dee said.

"Just ignore them," I told him. "They don't know anything."

Shelby came out with more ice cream, and all the kids started trying to grab it off the tray and the moms had to forget about us and yell at the kids. When Shelby saw who my friend was, his head jerked back. He finished with the ice cream, set down his tray, and straightened up his tall back and came to our table.

I thought he might say it was high time his people ate there, or at least smile and ask what we wanted to drink. But he wasn't smiling. He was looking concerned. Very concerned.

"This is my friend Dee," I said.

"Hello, Dee," Shelby said.

"Hey, Mr. Shelby," said Dee, looking at the carpet.

"Wait a minute," I said, "y'all know each other? This is great!"

"Dee, does your mama know about this?"

"No, sir."

Shelby leaned down to Dee and said, in a voice as gentle as a doctor's, "Son, you know you can't be in here."

Dee looked down and didn't say anything.

"We'd like two cheeseburgers and log fries, please," I said. "What do you want to drink, Dee?"

Shelby acted like he hadn't heard me.

"Y'all need to run on, Mr. Trip."

"What? Why?"

He just looked at me. Then he said, "I'm gonna have to get Mr. Lonnie," and turned around and left.

"It's gonna be okay," I told Dee.

"No it's not. Mr. Shelby is an elder in my church. Mama's gonna kill me."

Mr. Lonnie hustled out to our table like a fat baseball player trying to get onto the field. I knew what he was about to say, and I had not pedaled a bike all the way to the Golliwog to hear it. If I could find

Papaw, he'd tell Mr. Lonnie to hustle right back to the kitchen.

"Boys, the dining room is closed for a private party. Y'all are gonna have to eat lunch someplace else today." His voice was sharp and proud of itself.

"Come on." Dee was standing up.

"Sit down, Dee. Shelby said y'all were open." I said it pretty loud. The moms and cone hats stopped talking and stared at us.

"Well, Shelby was wrong. Let's go."

Mr. Lonnie tried to pull my chair away from the table, but I grabbed the seat and wouldn't budge. I felt that monster getting into me. I was mad enough to do something crazy, something like make a scene at the club. Dee was shaking his head at me. I looked at him and Mr. Lonnie and turned to everybody and said,

"This is my guest. His name is Dee. And we would like some cheeseburgers!"

One of the moms I didn't know said, "Let the boys have lunch, Lonnie. What's the big deal?" The other moms frowned at her.

Mr. Lonnie leaned over me and said in a voice only I was supposed to hear, "Son, if you and your little colored friend don't get outta here right now, you're gonna be in big trouble, you hear me?"

I've been taught all my life to be respectful to grown-ups, and I knew I was not being respectful now.

I stood up and stretched my face to where I could look him real good in the eye.

"Just tell me why," I said.

"Out!"

"Tell me why!"

He turned red and started yelling.

When I turned back around, Dee was gone. I ran after him so fast, I accidentally knocked Mr. Lonnie against the wall. The moms gasped and chattered. Mr. Lonnie was still yelling when I cleared the top of the stairs.

Dee was already sitting on his bike.

"I'm really sorry," I told him. "I didn't know it would be like that."

"Why didn't you know?" He said the words in slow motion.

He walked his wheels over the curb and took off. Riding single file with all that traffic made it hard to talk, and he didn't want to talk anyway. It was a long trip back.

I figured everything would be okay between us as soon as we got something to eat and he felt better and would listen to me. He would understand that I was trying to do something good. He got way ahead of me toward the end. When I turned onto Oak Lane Drive, he was already dropping the bike. When I got to the kitchen, he was sitting at the table with a big bowl of macaroni and cheese and didn't look up when I came in. I didn't want to talk about it with Willie Jane around. We couldn't talk much anyway; we about had our faces in the bowls. When we were through with that bowlful, we ate another one. Dee had three.

He didn't have to leave for another couple of hours, so I said we oughta go out back and throw the football. I was holding my breath and hoping he wouldn't say, "Why don't we throw it out front?" He just said okay.

After we had tossed it back and forth a couple of times, I said, "Look, Dee, like I said, I'm sorry. I didn't expect it to be like that."

"How did you expect it to be?" He threw it back harder than usual.

"I don't know. . . . My papaw said if I brought a Negro to the Golliwog, he would buy him lunch."

"And you needed a Negro to help you prove it."

"I wanted you to be able to get something to eat. If you're my guest, you have a right to eat in there as much as anybody else. If I could've found Papaw, I bet—"

"Things are the way they are! When Mr. Shelby tells my mama about this, I'm gonna be in all kinds of trouble—thanks to you!"

He threw the ball so hard, it hurt to catch it. I slung it back just as hard.

"I'll explain it to your mama. You want me to go explain it to her right now?"

"No, I'm gonna explain something to *you*. You can't mess with me like that! I am *not* your pet nigger to show off to the white people!"

He threw the ball at me like you would throw a rock at somebody and started walking up to the house. Then he turned around and yelled, "I'm not even your friend!" and kept walking.

When I asked Willie Jane where Dee had gone, she said he was sitting in the car. I asked her if he was okay, and she said she didn't know. She looked like she wanted to ask why he was sitting in the car, but then she looked like she knew that something bad was bound to happen and went back to ironing, like she was angry at the shirt. I had let her down. She had trusted me to take care of her boy.

I looked out the front window and saw Dee sitting there. I was sorry about everything, and almost went out there to apologize, but I was mad, too. I had been trying to do something nice for him—he didn't have any right to act like that. I went back to my room and lay down on my bed and stared at the ceiling, still feeling shaky. My "pet nigger"? I had never thought of Dee that way. That wasn't why I took him to the club. I didn't do it for me. It wasn't like I was trying to show off.

Was I?

Well, it was done now, and maybe I was the stupidest kid in the world. Maybe that was the problem. How many people had gotten mad at me today? It had to be some kind of record.

Mama tromped back to my room in those high-heeled shoes that make such a racket, and stood there with her hands on her hips and her eyes flashing black. The dread came up in my throat. I had been trying to figure out how to tell her, but the ladies at the bridge tournament beat me to it.

Daddy wouldn't have been so mad, and I could have thought straight and explained it better. Mama says Daddy is such a smart man, and that he's taught her to have a more "open-minded" way of looking at things. Well, I didn't see how she could be all open-minded and still get so mad.

"Is it true?" she asked.

"Is what true?"

"Don't you play games with me, young man. Did you take Dee to the Golliwog? Did you push Mr. Lonnie against a wall?"

"That was an accident. Listen, Mama, Papaw said if I brought an upstanding Negro to the Golliwog, he would buy him lunch, and I just wanted to show everybody that—that—"

"That what? That you enjoy disgracing your family?"

Her being so mad made me mad, and I just came out with the whole thing.

"I did not disgrace my family! Do you know what the word 'golliwog' means? Why'd they name it that? It's ugly. I'm never going back. I'm never goin' to that country club again!" I said it louder than I meant to.

Mama held out her hands and took a deep breath to show how we both needed to calm down. Then she smiled the "you know so well that I am right" smile and talked extra quiet to show me how I, especially, needed to calm down.

"Black people don't eat lunch or play golf or go swimming at the club because that's the way it has been since before you or I were born, and you need to honor the wisdom of your elders. There's such a thing as tradition, Trip. I just pray your grandparents don't hear about this."

"What if it's a bad tradition?"

"You can decide about what's a bad tradition when you're grown. Things are a lot more complicated than you are able to realize at your age. Until then, you will follow the rules of civilized society."

She started to walk out and turned around.

"Really, Trip! I can't imagine what you were thinking, riding your bike all that way in Old Canton Road traffic—"

"Actually, Dee rode my bike, and I rode—"

"I don't care which bike you rode!"

"Willie Jane said it was okay."

"Willie Jane should have known better. You've gotten her in trouble, too. We'll decide on your punishment when your father gets home."

When Daddy came home, they went back and talked about me in their bedroom, but she was the only one who came into my room later and told me my punishment: Grounded for three weeks with no TV—and Dee could not come over anymore. I didn't tell her the real punishment was that Dee didn't *want* to come over anymore.

Mama was still mad the next morning, all through the cheese grits. I showed her how shiny my shoes were for church, and she didn't care one bit. Farish saw something was wrong and wouldn't leave me alone about it, so I finally told her what happened.

"You rode my bike without my permission?" She loves a reason to fuss.

"You weren't here for me to ask permission. I didn't have a choice anyway. We only have two bikes. You better not tell anybody about this either."

"I won't."

"Cross your heart and hope to die?"

"Cross my heart and hope to die."

Tim and Tom and their friends were sitting across the aisle and down a row at church, looking back at me and whispering—probably about all the ways they were going to beat me up. I just paid real good attention to Dr. Mercer's sermon on the poor widow and her mite and acted like I didn't even know they were there. After the service, I didn't look around for them on the way down the long front steps. I just looked straight ahead and walked slow and calm, like I wasn't worried about anything. Then I heard Mr. Bethune's voice and turned around.

"I wish I knew what y'all are thinking, letting your son invite colored boys to play football. You start lettin' 'em act like they belong in white society, and where's it gonna end? I didn't fight the Nazis and watch men die so we could have—"

Daddy went off like a bomb.

"That boy is not hurting anybody! The problem is that so many people around here are so ignorant and mean!"

I had never seen him get mad that fast. Not at another grown-up. His cheeks were bright red.

"And I'm saying *you're* the problem," said Mr. Bethune with his teeth together. He stood there while we kept going down the steps.

It was good to get to the bottom of those long steps and be on the way to dinner at Meemaw and Papaw's. Pretty soon, our plates were piled up with country-fried steak and gravy; biscuits; green beans and field peas cooked together with bacon, Meemaw-style; tomato casserole; and blackberry cobbler with homemade vanilla ice cream on top.

The Rebels had tied Vanderbilt 7–7, so there was that to talk about. I didn't care what we talked about, as long as it wasn't about me. Mama smiled and said what a sunshiny day it was, but she was worried under her smile.

Meemaw started in about the terrible things she had heard about Kansas City and how she could not imagine why anybody would want to move to a big Yankee city like that. Papaw said he had heard about Southern children getting fussed at by their teachers there for saying "yes, ma'am." Meemaw said the people there had funny accents and were not nearly as good-looking as Southerners. Did they want their son to marry some Yankee girl and give them ugly grandchildren?

Mama and Daddy were real quiet and acting like their chairs were too hard. I tried to think of something to say about church or school to change the subject. Nothing came to me, but I jumped in anyway.

"Meemaw? Meemaw?" It came out too loud.

"What, honey?"

"Um . . . that decorated pumpkin thing in the middle of the table, is that for Halloween?"

"Oh, it's just part of my harvest theme. Haven't you noticed all my harvest décor around the house?"

"Yes, ma'am, looks real good," I said, which was sort of a lie since I wasn't clear on what "décor" was. "I thought it might be for Halloween. Do y'all get very many trick-or-treaters?"

"Oh yes, we get quite a few."

"Us too. Will you be making special Halloween cookies like last year, or anything?"

"I 'spect I will." She made the same tight lips and big eyes Mama does when I'm supposed to get all excited about something.

That was all I could think of to say about Halloween and she was right back on Kansas City again. Mama explained that it was just a possibility that she and Daddy thought they ought to look into, and Daddy said his friend Glen was such a wonderful guy and a great doctor. They were both stiff and talking soft at first, but they got louder.

Then Papaw finally said something about the Rebel game, and by the time Meemaw brought out the blackberry cobbler and ice cream, things had calmed down a little, at least for me. We were all the way to dessert, and it looked like the grandparents didn't know what happened yesterday at the country club. I knew Mama wasn't going to bring it up. Then Farish said, "By the way, did you hear what happened yesterday when Trip took Willie Jane's little boy to the country club?"

If Mama could have reached that far across the table, she would have stuck her fork in Farish's forehead.

Farish smiled at me and showed me her fingers under the table. Dangit! I forgot to say "No crosses count." It wasn't that she was still mad about me riding her bike without permission, it was just such an easy way to get me in trouble.

"What?" Meemaw looked at Farish like she had said something in Chinese.

"Trip and his colored friend tried to have cheeseburgers in the Golliwog," Farish said. "They got kicked out, though."

"His colored friend!" said Meemaw.

I wasn't trying to exactly blame it on Papaw, but I had to explain it:

"Papaw said if I knew a colored person who was hungry, to bring him to the club and he'd buy him lunch."

Meemaw looked hard at Papaw. I've only seen her call him by his name, Bill, when we come back too late from fishing at Ratliff's pond.

"Bee-yul?"

"What's that?" Papaw looked real confused.

"I looked for you, Papaw, but I couldn't find you," I said. "I knew you'd say it was okay."

Everybody was frozen solid—except for Farish, who smiled at me like she just adored her big brother, and Ginny Lynn, who was digging into her cobbler and never knows what's going on anyway.

Finally, Papaw said, "I think I did say something like that to Trip the other day. We were havin' a conversation about the Negroes." He looked at me and laughed a little. "I didn't know he would take immediate action on it. Nothing to get woiked up about, though, just a little miscommunication. Right, partnuh?" He winked at me.

"My stars," Meemaw said. "How in the world—?"

"I'm sure Trip didn't mean to do anything wrong." Mama gave Farish the black-eyed glare.

"No, ma'am. I sure didn't," I said.

Nobody said anything.

Then Daddy said, "I think Trip was trying to do a good thing—maybe he didn't do it the right way, but a good thing."

Nobody talked.

Then Papaw said, "To bring Negroes to lunch is a good thing? I suppose those Negroes trying to eat lunch at Walgreens last year were also doing a *good* thing?"

"Y'all, please . . . ," Mama said.

"Maybe they were," Daddy said. "Sitting there for hours with a bunch of idiots yelling at them and pouring salt and sugar and mustard on them . . . I mean, they clearly believe in what they're doing. Medgar Evers shot dead in his driveway . . ."

"I see," Papaw said, but he didn't sound like he wanted to see.

Meemaw said, "Well, I swan," and nodded and looked hard at Daddy like she always knew he would say something like that.

"Y'all finish up, children," Mama said.

"Martin Luther King . . . ," Daddy said.

"Martin Luther King! *Time* magazine's Man of the Year!" Papaw smiled real big. It wasn't a real smile.

Mama begged Daddy with her eyes. Meemaw said something to her plate. Then all you could hear was chewing.

I wanted so bad to explain to Meemaw why I took Dee to the club, but I didn't want to give her a heart attack. Anyway, I've heard Daddy say you can't explain anything to Meemaw, that she lives in her own special world.

"You see what you did?" I pinched Farish's arm on the way to the car. She knew better than to complain to Mama, too. Mama was more outdone with her than me now and would have been glad to pinch her other arm. We got on the backseat with Ginny Lynn between us.

"Well, that was certainly a delightful meal and loads of fun," Daddy said, like an announcer on TV.

"I didn't think it was that much fun," Farish whispered to me.

"He's being sarcastic," I told her.

All the way home it was that thick, terrible quiet when something is all your fault.

"Do you hate Mississippi?" I said to Farish, trying to whisper.

"No."

"I do."

Mama heard. "Trip Westbrook, your mother's side of the family has lived in Mississippi for two hundred years."

"Does that mean *we* have to?"

"I don't want to move to Kansas City, I'll tell you that," Farish said.

"Y'all have both said enough for one day. Just hush."

I changed out of my scratchy suit when we got home and made sure the creases were together on the pants when I hung them up. Then I went down to the creek. The water was pretty low and I thought maybe I could spot that snake. Stokes says they've all gone into hibernation by now, but I still had this feeling it was around somewhere. I walked from the pine stump at one end of the yard to the bridge at the other. Nothing out there but a lizard.

Mama fixed salmon croquettes for supper, which I love. Her mood had definitely changed.

Daddy said the blessing, which is always exactly the same: "Dear God, we thank you for this food. Bless it to the nourishment of our bodies and us to thy service. In Jesus's name. Amen." If he ever needs me to fill in, I'm ready.

He said he was tired of trying to talk Dr. Freeman and the other doctors into getting rid of the separate waiting room for colored patients. He said that situation, along with everything else, was about to send him over the edge.

"Where will you be when you're over the edge?" I asked.

"Crazy."

Word got around at school about my colored friend. People kept their distance like I had a special disease. But Miss Hooper looked at me like she never noticed me before and was so glad I was in her class.

She was telling us about Ponce de León and the Fountain of Youth and somehow started talking about Roderick, the one colored kid who goes to our school. She said it was time everybody was nicer to him. He's the first one ever to go here. I've been trying to figure out why he would want to.

Bobby Watson raised his hand and asked why it was even okay for him to be here.

"Because it's *the law*! We've been over this!" Nancy Harper said, like she was the teacher.

"Y'all need to be nice to Roderick," Miss Hooper said. "I mean normal nice. I see people treating him like the school mascot or somethin'. Just be real to him."

I know people who flat-out hate Roderick for being here and want him gone. I bet they're "real" to him when nobody's looking.

"It would be nice if y'all took the initiative to sit by Roderick at lunch and try to get to know him a little bit. He's doing a brave thing being here, probably braver than any of us would ever do."

Bobby Watson raised his hand again: "Maybe Trip could take him to lunch at the country club," which made everybody laugh except me and Nancy and Miss Hooper.

Miss Hooper looked hard at Bobby and said, "Maybe he could," like she was taking him seriously. Then her eyes went to the back of the room, right to me, and stayed there. I knew what that meant.

I'm not afraid to talk in class, but I sure didn't want to talk about what happened with Dee. All I could think was Please no, please no, please no. . . .

"Trip?"

"Yes, ma'am?" Pleasenopleasenopleaseno . . .

"I wonder if you would be willing to share your recent experience with the class? I know I'd like to hear about it. I think everyone would benefit from hearing what happened."

She looked at them like they all needed to learn something, and here I was, teacher's special prize, ready to teach it to them. I almost asked her if she was willing to be my friend now and hang out with me, because after this nobody else would.

"Well, I mean, my maid's son, Dee . . . uh, he plays football with us, me and Stokes and Andy and the guys. . . ."

But Stokes and Andy don't have history that period. I was all on my own.

"Stand up and tell us."

"Ma'am?"

"Stand up. I want to make sure everybody hears." She frowned at Bobby.

"Well, uh, my papaw said he'd buy a colored person lunch if they were hungry, and I don't know, I thought it would be okay to take Dee to the club for a cheeseburger."

They were already snickering and whispering. Miss Hooper was smiling at me like I was some kind of angel.

"And what happened?"

"They told us to get out. They said it was closed for a party. Not at first."

"And how did that make you feel?"

"It made me mad and then Dee got mad at me and . . . Miss Hooper, do I have to talk about this?"

"That's okay, Trip. Thank you."

I sat down and took a big breath. My fingers were trembling.

Miss Hooper looked around to make sure the lesson had been learned, and went back to Ponce de León. I thought she would say how brave I was or something. I bet there are rules on how much a teacher can say, even Miss Hooper, if she wants to stay a teacher.

It was hot and sticky outside. The sky was solid white and hung right in my eyes. Roderick sat on the low wall in front of the school, away from the after-lunch crowd, looking like he wished somebody would rescue him from this place. I told myself I would go up and talk to him and be real, like Miss Hooper said—just not today.

Then Nancy pulled herself up on the wall and started talking to him. I couldn't let her beat me. I went over there and sat on Roderick's other side.

"How's it goin'?" I said.

He nodded.

"Tell Trip what you were just telling me." Nancy leaned forward and looked at me. "You are not going to believe this."

Roderick didn't seem too sure about talking to me.

"It's okay. I have a colored friend," I said.

"Really?"

"We play football together. I took him to the country club."

He smiled. "So you're the one, huh?"

"I'm the one."

"Be careful. You don't want to push too hard. What I was telling Nancy, my mama's worked at Remington's downtown for twelve years, and when she went in last Monday they told her she doesn't have a job anymore."

"Why not?"

"They said it was because she was letting colored ladies try on hats, but she's been doin' that a long time—what it is, they found out I go to this school. I told her I like comin' here but I didn't want her to lose her job because of me."

"You really like it?" I didn't see how he could.

"I mean, I don't like being the only colored kid, but this is so much better than my other school. My other school didn't even have enough books for everybody. They didn't even have enough chalk for the blackboard."

"Maybe your mom can find a place to work with better people," Nancy said.

"Maybe. My daddy's a dentist, and a man called the house last week and said I better go back to the school where I belong or they were going to blow up his clinic. And the last few days, three white men in a Chevrolet have been stoppin' in front of my house."

"Why?"

"Maybe they want to blow the house up too, I don't know. But they stay out there."

"Have y'all called the police?"

"Police would bring 'em refreshments."

"You should get a bunch of guys together and go out there and tell them to get the heck off your street," I said. "I'll help you."

"Oh, come on," Nancy said. She said "on" "ahn."

"I will," I said.

Roderick looked like he believed me. I think I even believed me. People were staring at us when they walked by, but I didn't care. I didn't even care if the Bethunes saw us: the Yankee girl, the colored guy, and me.

When I was a little kid, I had a color for every day of the week. Monday was orange, the worst color. Tuesday was green. Wednesday was unlucky yellow, like certain dog doo. Thursday was light blue because it was almost Friday, Friday was blue like the sky, and Saturday was the deepest blue. Sunday was golden for the Lord.

If the little kid version of me walked in here right now, I would tell him, "Listen, stupid, you don't get to say what kind of day it's going to be. Wednesdays are not always unlucky, and Saturdays are not always that great, no matter what color you give them. You don't get to have control over the days of the week or much else. It's all a lot messier than you want it to be. When you're twelve, LSU is going to beat Ole Miss 11–10 on Halloween, and that's not the scariest thing that's going to happen."

That night the phone started ringing and wouldn't stop. For some reason nobody in the house would answer it. I ran into the den and grabbed it.

"Hello?"

There was some kind of quick, muffled talk, not into the phone. Then nothing.

"Hello?"

Nothing.

I hung up.

Mama came into the room with her robe half-buttoned and her hair all messed up.

"Who was it?"

"I don't know. They wouldn't say anything."

"Wouldn't say anything?"

"How come I'm the only one who can answer a telephone around here, anyway?" I asked her, but she was already halfway back down the hall.

When I got home from school the next afternoon, Willie Jane had *The Secret Storm* blaring all over the playroom. It's one of her "stories" she always watches when she irons. Farish and Ginny Lynn were sitting in front of the TV, ignoring a pile of pick-up sticks. I am 100 percent positive they don't understand soap operas, but they sat there anyway, staring with their mouths open.

"Where's your mama?" asked Willie Jane.

"Mama went on to the Sunflower after she let me out."

"You don't want to help your mama buy groceries?"

"Very funny."

"You sure don't mind eatin' 'em, though."

I nodded. Then I said, "Farish! Come on and throw me some passes."

"I'm busy."

"Busy doing nothin'."

"I'm watching this."

"That's a bunch of junk."

"Don't you be talkin' about my stories," said Willie Jane.

The phone rang.

"There it goes again," Willie Jane said.

"What?"

"I've been runnin' to that phone all day, and soon as I say 'Westbrook residence,' they hang up. They do it every time."

"They did it to me last night."

"I *wish* there was a way to tell who's callin' you on the phone. With everything they're comin' up with these days, I wish they could come up with that. People ain't got nothin' better to do than try and scare us with the phone?"

"Nobody's trying to scare us, Willie Jane. Let me answer it."

I had to prove to myself that nothing weird was going on, probably just some idiot dialing the wrong number. If I fooled them with my voice, they might get too confused to call anymore. I was trying for chief of police, but it came out more Englishy, like somebody's butler.

"Halllooo?"

Willie Jane laughed.

"Tree-up?"

"Meemaw!"

"Hey, sweetheart! Is ya mama home?"

I could see Meemaw holding the phone against her ear with her shoulder, fiddling with her nails and smiling while she talked. It was the most beautiful smile in the world.

I handed Willie Jane the phone and let her tell Meemaw when Mama would be home.

"See?" I said when she hung up. "Now you can relax."

"I hope you're right."

The phone rang again. We looked at each other.

"It's probably Meemaw again," I said. "Something she forgot to tell us."

R-i-i-i-i-ng!

"You answer it then," she said.

R-i-i-i-i-ng!

I picked it up.

"Hello?"

Nothing.

"Hello?"

Nothing.

I was about to put the receiver down when a voice said,

"You better watch your back, nigger lover."

It was a flat, cold voice, like somebody who had crawled out of the woods to find a phone just so he could threaten me. How did that voice know my telephone number?

"Leave us alone!" I yelled into the phone and slammed it down.

"Did they say something? What did they say?" Willie Jane grabbed my arm.

I didn't want to tell her what he said, but she made me repeat it word for word.

"Who was it?" she asked. "Bethune boys?"

"I don't know."

I ran to the living room windows and looked out, almost expecting to see a dirty-looking man under the streetlight with a phone in one hand and a gun in the other. I pulled the curtains on all the front windows. Then I ran back to the den and pulled the curtain over the sliding glass door.

That night, Mama and Daddy got into an argument, which almost never happens. They were loud and talked about us like we weren't there. Mama wanted to call the police right away. It was her angry voice but scared, too, which I had not heard before. I was sorry I had told her how the voice on the phone scared me.

"To call the police would be an overreaction," Daddy said. "It's probably just kids. Or some of Pete Bethune's redneck buddies who don't know their hind ends from a hole in the ground."

"They are terrorizing our children, Sam!"

"We should play it cool and give whoever it is a chance to get bored. They will."

Mama tromped back to her room.

Daddy sat, looked around and saw us, and told Ginny Lynn to get up in his lap. He gave her a hug and said not to be worried or scared about this phone business. We were just going to have to wait it out and not answer any calls ever. He or Mama would answer the phone at night, in case it was a patient or somebody from the hospital.

After supper I got through as much homework as I could stand and was trying to go to sleep when Mama came in and sat on the bed.

"Honey, I've thought about it and I wanted to tell you I'm sorry for getting so upset about you taking Dee to the club. I know you were trying to do something good, like your daddy says. You just went about it the wrong way. You see that, don't you?"

"Yes, ma'am. Good night."

147

"Are you sure you see?" She raised her eyebrow like she thought I was hiding something. I just wanted to go to sleep.

"Yes, ma'am. It's against tradition."

"That's right. Trip, you don't really hate your home state, do you?"

"Doesn't Daddy hate it?"

"He . . . definitely gets *impatient* with it." She sighed and looked like she wasn't sure she should tell me this. "Your daddy says he's been trying to drag me out from behind the 'magnolia curtain' ever since we met. Well, I'm getting there. I never knew he meant *physically* drag me until all this talk about Kansas City."

" 'Magnolia curtain'?"

"The old-fashioned way of life that separates us from the rest of the country."

"Way of life like Jim Crow?"

"Yes. There is such a thing as a bad tradition, like you said. I know Mississippi is gonna have to change, but when you've grown up a certain way, it's hard to rethink everything . . . especially when life has been good to you the way it has to us."

"But not so good if you're colored."

"No."

"And you don't have anything, and you can't do anything."

"We need to fix that, we do. It will take time."

"I guess it doesn't matter anyway if we're movin'."

"We'll wait and see about that."

She kissed me on the forehead and said good night.

I stayed awake a long time, thinking about it. Part of me still wants to get away from these yahoos. But most of me can't even think about living anywhere else.

I don't know what the age limit is on trick-or-treating, but twelve must be close, because putting on a costume and going around begging for candy didn't seem that great to me. I was more excited about the fact that Ole Miss was playing LSU. But I found some jeans with holes in them and an old red-checked shirt, and Mama made me a pouch out of a scrap of cloth, and we filled it with newspaper and tied it to the end of a long stick for me to carry. I got Mama's straw yard hat from the storage room and there was my hobo outfit. Or Huckleberry Finn outfit. I just didn't feel like being scary this year. Real life was scary enough.

Stokes was a vampire, supposedly. All he did was wear fake teeth and slick his hair straight back. I thought it would be me and him and Andy and Calvin, but Stokes said Andy and Calvin had decided at the last minute to go to another neighborhood. It took a while to cover the three main streets of Oakwood. Sometimes people would open the door smiling, then see me and stop smiling and throw candy in our bags like they couldn't wait to shut the door. I asked Stokes if it seemed like people weren't as friendly as they used to be. He said I was right, they weren't. Maybe they thought we were too old, especially with Stokes being so tall now.

When we got back to the house, Mama said she was disappointed with the turnout this year. Halloween is right up there with Christmas for her. She strung giant spiderwebs in the bushes and bought extra Kraft caramels and chocolates and everything. She carved an extra pumpkin so we could have two, one smiley, one scary. This neighborhood's so full of kids, she said she couldn't believe more of them didn't come to our house.

Me and Stokes ate candy and listened to the Rebels lose—by one point. We spend the night at each other's houses all the time, but after the game, he said he had to go, that his mom wanted him home for some reason. I went on to bed. Daddy likes to say, "I've enjoyed about as much of this as I can stand." That's how I felt about Halloween this year.

Farish woke me up, tugging on my arm.

"Trip, wake up! They wrote all over the house!"

"Who wrote?"

"Bad words. Mama's going crazy! Come on!"

I put on my robe. Mama was stomping up and down the porch.

"Trip, do you know anything about this?"

"No, ma'am!" I couldn't believe she asked me that. I guess she was just that desperate to find out who did it.

Daddy was looking off down the street with his arms folded.

Ginny Lynn pointed to the front windows and said, "Look, Trip, look!" like a fun surprise had happened.

The windows would be easy to clean off. They were all scrawled over in soap with terrible things. Every window, top and bottom. Over on the shingles past the porch was a giant LOSER in black spray paint. First, I thought about how we would never get that off the house. Then I knew they were talking about Ole Miss losing to LSU and I knew who had done it. I would be sitting in church with them later that morning.

They wrote GO BACK TO AFRICA! in white spray paint on the garage. That one made me the angriest because it was about Dee, who was my friend whether he thought so or not.

"Call the police, Sam," Mama said.

"I'm not gonna call the police about a Halloween prank."

"This is more than a Halloween prank! They have ruined the front of our house! What are you saying, we just stand around and wait for whatever's next?"

"I'm saying I'll take care of it."

She strained up to his face and yelled, "Call the police! Or you'll have a crazy wife to take care of!"

She started crying, grabbed the girls, and went inside.

Daddy said we had time to wash the soap off the windows, but the other would have to wait. He was too mad to say anything else. When we had finished with the windows, I told him it might be a good day to stay home from church. He said no, it was more important than ever to go to church so we could ask God to forgive whoever did this, that somebody needed to forgive them. I guess he meant he couldn't.

After church, we tried scrubbing the paint with turpentine. You could still read the words, only now the letters were smeared, so it looked a lot worse. Daddy said we would have to call some painters. Tim and Tom weren't in Sunday School, but after lunch I saw them come by our house in their dad's beat-up white truck and slow down and look at each other and laugh. You can get your learner's permit when you're fourteen and a half. You're supposed to have an adult in the car with you, though, and they drive around all the time by themselves.

When I told Daddy I had just seen the Bethunes drive by and laugh at our house, a dark cloud moved over his face, and he said, "Maybe I'll call the police after all." He held up his hand for me to stay out on the porch, but when I heard him on the phone in the den, I stepped inside and listened.

". . . and I'm telling you we can't answer our phone

because these people are calling the house at all hours and hanging up. They even threatened my son. On the phone. Yes. And now they have painted 'Loser' and 'Go back to Africa' all over the front of my house. Yes, I'm white. It's directed at my maid's son. No. And they wrote racial epithets with soap all over the windows. Epithets. Insulting words. Yes. I know last night was Halloween, but these are the same people who have been calling and hanging up. . . ."

"Trip?"

"Aaahh!"

Farish was right behind me.

"Go away!" I whispered as loud as I could and still be whispering.

Of course she had to stand there too now and wouldn't go away, and I didn't want to make any more noise by arguing with her. I was pretty sure Daddy had heard me scream, but he was still talking.

"Look, is there a way to find out who it is? About a week ago, I guess. Well, we just thought we'd be able to handle it but after— No, I am not going to change my phone to a private number! I'm a doctor, for God's sake, people have to know how to reach me. Yes. Well, I know it's not a simple thing. There *is* a pattern of criminal activity, I just told you. . . . Yes. . . . Dr. Sam Westbrook. Fifty-four forty-five Oak Lane Drive. All right. Good-bye."

I pushed Farish toward her room and ran to the

bathroom and flushed the toilet and came out when I heard Daddy walking down the hall.

"Did you call 'em?" I asked.

"They're sending somebody over."

Daddy talked to the policeman on the porch. When he was gone, Daddy told us that just like he thought, the cops weren't going to be much help. He said there was no way to trace hang-up calls because they weren't staying on the line, and we had no real proof of who defaced the house, so there wasn't much to be done about that either. The police said to report any further problems.

It was a terrible word, "defaced." Our house used to have a face and they *de*-faced it.

Daddy told Mama about talking to Mr. Bethune. He had claimed not to know anything about any writing on our house. He said his whole family had stayed home on Halloween.

The painters painted over the writing. But the phone wouldn't stop ringing, and we didn't know what would happen next. Mama's eyes looked worried all the time now, which made the girls worried too. Mama said we didn't need to scare them by talking about it.

My stomach jumped now whenever I saw a white truck or heard the crack of a .22 from over in the woods. Tim and Tom were probably just shooting at bottles or squirrels and blue jays. It might not have even been their gun I was hearing, but shooting inside the city limits was against the law, and I didn't think there could be that many people around here who didn't care about the law.

Two weeks later, it was kind of a relief when we came back from Sunday lunch at Morrison's and found our mailbox lying around in pieces. At least now I knew what the next thing was.

We had gone straight to lunch after church, so it could have happened any time between about nine-thirty and one-thirty. Me and Daddy went next door to the Cargyles' to see if they had seen anything. Mr. Cargyle and Stokes came to the door. They said the parents had gone to church and let Stokes and Andy stay home, and they had heard the explosion but didn't see who did it. Stokes acted like he didn't really want to talk to me. I figured it was because he had invited Andy to spend the night instead of me.

Then we went to ask the Nelsons, Mrs. Sitwell, and the Cooks. Nobody had seen or heard anything and nobody smiled and nobody wanted to talk to us.

This time a different policeman came to the house. I told him it had to be the Bethunes because Tim and Tom loved to set off cherry bombs. He said it looked like a lot more than a cherry bomb, that it was probably some kind of Drano bomb or something. He looked around the yard and asked Daddy if he wanted them to talk to Mr. Bethune again and Daddy said no, that it wouldn't do any good and he would handle it. The policeman told him to be careful how he handled it. And to report any further problems.

When they were driving off, I asked Daddy why the policeman had told him to be careful when it was our mailbox that got blown up.

"They don't want me to do anything illegal," he said.

"Of course you're not gonna do anything illegal."

"If it comes right down to it, I might."

Mama and Daddy never said they blamed me. I would have felt better if they had just come out and said it: "This is *your fault*." When Farish said it, I raised my hand like I was gonna swat her, but I didn't. All I ever wanted was for Dee to do the same things with me my other friends do. I guess I went about it the wrong way, like Mama said. But what was the right way?

This trouble people were giving us was pointless. Dee hated my guts. Maybe they'd leave us alone if I put up signs all over north Jackson: YOU CAN RELAX. TRIP WESTBROOK DOES NOT HAVE A COLORED FRIEND ANYMORE. Maybe then life could get back to normal. But I wouldn't feel normal until he *was* my friend again.

I've been telling Willie Jane how bad I feel about

what happened with Dee. I found her ironing in the playroom and asked her again to bring him back over.

"Trip, I told you so many times. Dee's better off at home, with all this stuff goin' on."

"What about the fact that I really want him to come over?"

She set down the iron and looked around the playroom like she was seeing it for the last time.

"Pretty soon it won't matter anyway. Y'all about to go off and leave me. I heard your mama talking about Kansas City."

"Mama doesn't want to move to Kansas City any more than I do. Why should we let 'em run us off, is what I say. I'm not scared."

"You should be scared. I know what some kinds of white people will do. Dr. Westbrook has to keep y'all safe."

"If we do move, you and Dee can come with us."

She shook her head. "I don't expect that's gonna happen."

"I could ask Daddy to move y'all up there with us, get you a house and everything."

"No you couldn't."

"Wouldn't you rather be in a better place for colored people? And you would still have us. I mean, I don't want to leave Mississippi, but I don't know why a colored person would want to stay here."

"Same reason as you. It's home. You take the bad

157

with the good. Anyway, it costs too much to get out. If I did, I 'spect I'd miss it. But I wouldn't mind findin' out for sure." She smiled.

"If we move, you'll get the chance to find out."

"No, no, no, you just leave that alone." She started ironing again. "My brothers got out. One went to St. Louis and one to Detroit. Dee's daddy used to talk about when he would move us all up North. He wanted to get away so bad."

"What happened?"

"I think wanting it so bad for so long and not getting it . . . it finally drove him crazy. He quit his job. He quit caring about things."

"Willie Jane, especially if we move, I have to see Dee again."

She set down the iron again.

"Child, it makes me happy you want to see him so bad. You keep on about it so much, I guess I'm gonna have to tell you the truth." She lit a cigarette and looked at me like she had so much to say, she couldn't say it all. "Dee doesn't want to come over here. He says too many bad things happen when he's here."

"He had fun with us, I know he did."

"He did have fun with you, playing football and all, but he doesn't think you did him right, taking him to the white people's club."

"But I was trying to do something good. I need a

chance to make him see that. That's why he has to come over, so I can explain. I feel so"—something hot rushed up into my eyes and made them clench—"so bad about everything." I ran the back of my hand over my face.

"I know you do, darlin'. I'm past fussin' at you about it, but you know you got me in trouble that day, too."

"I know. I'm sorry." My eyes wouldn't stay open. "Tell him. Please. He can come over at least one more time."

"I'll tell him, but you better not count on it. You better learn it now that the world doesn't want white boys and colored to be friends. And the older you get, the truer that's gonna be."

"One day it will be different. When I grow up, I'm gonna put a commercial on TV that says: 'Come to Mississippi: where anybody can be friends with anybody.'"

She laughed a little.

"I hope you do. I hope you do."

The phone kept ringing and only Mama and Daddy could answer it, and they were gone a lot, especially Daddy, so you just had to sit there and let it hurt your ears. Sometimes it was all day and sometimes only a few times that day, but it always rang at night. And as soon as you fell asleep, it would ring again. Daddy had to keep telling us that we could not change our number and keep it a secret, because the hospitals needed to be able to reach him.

"Anyway," he said. "We won't have to put up with hang-up calls or any of the rest of this bull crap much longer." I had never heard him say "bull crap" before.

Mama picked me up from school and made me go to the Sunflower with her because it was so much easier to drive to the grocery store from school than to take me home first, and she was too tired to argue about it. I was too tired to argue about it, too. I never got enough sleep anymore, even with a pillow wrapped around my ears.

We drove home with more paper sacks than would fit on the backseat. I had some serious unloading to do. Mama let me do it all, too. The only thing she carried into the house was her purse.

"Hey, Farish!" I yelled. "Help me get these grocery bags!"

"Farish can't carry those," Mama said.

"She can carry the lighter ones. Farish!"

We walked into the den and there was Farish sitting on the floor by the couch looking up at me, scared, with Ginny Lynn sitting right next to her.

"Why didn't you answer me?"

And there was Willie Jane sitting in the middle of the couch with Daddy's 12-gauge shotgun across her lap.

"What in the world . . . ?" Mama said.

"Ain't nobody gonna hurt my babies," said Willie Jane. "Ain't nobody gonna hurt my babies. . . ."

"Willie Jane?"

She looked like she did when we went after that snake. Her eyes were scary. I would not want to be on the wrong side of those eyes.

Ginny Lynn whimpered and jumped up and hugged Mama's legs.

"They talked this time, Miz Westbrook," Willie Jane said.

"What did they say?"

"They say better look out for the children, that they'd hate to see something happen to 'em. I almost fell out when I heard it."

Willie Jane wasn't sure about the voice. She said maybe it was a Bethune and maybe not. I wish I had been the one to answer it.

Daddy came home and said he could tell the police were not taking him seriously. He demanded to speak to someone higher up this time, and got hold of a detective. The detective told Daddy not to worry, that with us getting so many prank calls all the time, this had to be a prank call too. And Daddy should report any further problems.

He went over to the Bethunes' after supper. I wished

he had taken a gun. When he came back, his face was red and his eyes were hard as rocks. Mama acted like they ought to go back into their room to discuss it, but he was too mad to care if we heard.

"I told him to stop the calls."

"And?"

"Oh, he doesn't know anything about it! The liar. He was enjoying himself. He was having the time of his life. He's probably got his redneck buddies on call rotation."

"Did he deny making the threat?"

"He denied everything. I told him if he or his half-wit boys so much as looked cross-eyed at my family, I would come back over there and shoot him."

"Sam! No! Don't talk like that. I feel like I don't know you when you talk like that. We would leave it to the police if . . . if . . ."

"The police are worthless! How much more proof do you need of that?"

Farish was getting scared. I took her to the play-room and turned on the TV. Ginny Lynn was out there already playing with her Colorforms.

When I came back into the den, Daddy was saying he agreed with the detective that if anybody really wanted to hurt us, they wouldn't call and talk about it, they'd just do it. But we had to be careful.

"Let me go over there," I said. "I'll dare Tim and Tom to come outside. I'll tell them if they lay a finger on one of my sisters, I'll blast 'em with their own gun!"

"Of course you're not going over there, Trip."

"I would, though."

"I know you would." He smiled like he was proud of me. "But I don't even want you leaving the backyard."

"Aw, come on, Daddy!"

"Until further notice. I mean it."

"I don't want to be stuck in the backyard. I'm not afraid of those guys. I promised myself I wouldn't chicken out, and now you're making me."

"We need to know everybody's safe, pal."

He put his arm around my shoulder.

"Why can't we do something instead of sitting here and taking it?"

"We're doing everything we can."

"Can't walk around in my own neighborhood. On my own street. I am twelve and a half years old, for crying out loud."

"Old enough to understand why," Daddy said, and smiled like everything was going to be all right.

Farish and Ginny Lynn can't even go in the back-yard. Mama walks them to their classrooms in the morning and picks them up from their classrooms in the afternoon. Mama says Willie Jane's main job now is to watch them, even if some rugs don't get vacu-umed and some laundry doesn't get washed.

. . .

Daddy went to Kansas City for three days and when he came back, he said he had good news. He had found a house for us, a much bigger, better house, and we could move to Kansas City even sooner than he had hoped. The children had to help Mama and Willie Jane keep the house clean because it was time to get a real estate agent and start showing it to people. Soon there weren't gonna be any more people bothering us, he said, and everything was going to be great from now on.

I looked at Mama. How could she change her mind like this? She wouldn't look back at me, and then I knew that she had not changed her mind. She was "putting up a brave front," like she had told me to do. She didn't have a choice anymore. She was with Daddy, no matter what.

Daddy showed us pictures he had taken of the new house with his new Polaroid camera. It was bigger than our house, with a balcony across the front and a circular driveway. The living room looked huge and so did the kitchen. The den had a big brick fireplace and built-in bookshelves. And there was a giant brick patio in the back.

Farish said she didn't like that house. "What about Willie Jane?" she asked.

"We'll make sure Willie Jane has another family to work for," Daddy said.

"But we're her family."

"You can still visit her when we come home to see Meemaw and Papaw. She'll be fine."

"I just can't wait to plant some lantana all around that patio and jasmine on the trellis." Mama sounded like she was making herself say it. "Trip, you'll have to help me."

"Yes, ma'am."

"Are we running away from the bad people?" Ginny Lynn asked.

Mama sat up straighter.

"We aren't running away from anybody, honey," she said. "I want y'all to definitely understand that. We are moving to a better place. Daddy will have a better place to work, and we'll all have a better house, with more room for y'all to play in. The schools are a lot better, too."

"But we've always lived here," whined Ginny Lynn. "What's wrong with this house?"

"Nothing is wrong with this house, honey. But wouldn't you like a big house with an upstairs?"

"Will my room be bigger?" asked Farish.

"Everybody's room will be bigger."

"Will my room be bigger?" asked Ginny Lynn.

"Lots bigger," said Mama.

"Will it be upstairs?"

"Yes. Upstairs."

"Hmm. I'll think about it."

"Kansas City is a great town," Daddy said. "There's so much going on up there. We can go to the Athletics baseball games. Real professional baseball. Wouldn't that be fun?"

"Baseball is boring," Farish said.

"And, Trip, they have a new pro football team, the Chiefs."

"I know," I said, and tried to sound excited, even though I really like the NFL a lot more than the AFL.

"And Glen is a great guy," Daddy said. "He has a little girl seven years old. Farish, you would have an instant playmate."

"Y'all can move to Kansas City if you want to! I'm staying right here!" yelled Farish, and ran to her room.

The moving men were coming on Monday, only three days away. I would never live at 5445 Oak Lane Drive again. If I was ever going to get rid of that snake, that thing that had been alive in my head for almost two months, and maybe save the next kid who played in this backyard, it had to be now. I knew snakes were scarce in November, but I told myself maybe it might not be hibernating yet. Even though it was real cold earlier this week, it had turned warm again, and it had been mostly warm all fall.

I snuck up to the exact spot where I had seen it. My stomach clenched whenever I remembered almost touching it . . . but it wasn't there now. It had to be around here somewhere.

I held the hoe ready and walked from one end of the creek to the other, trying to see into the tallest grass at the edge without getting too close to it. I checked along the whole bank and didn't see anything. Then I checked it again, from the bridge all the way down to the big pine stump where Stokes's yard begins. All along the way, I swung the hoe into the grass near the water, where I couldn't see as good.

I stood there awhile staring at the creek, feeling dumb, but not willing to stop looking. I got so mad at the snake and mad at myself, I slammed the hoe into the top of that big old pine stump. It sank into the wood up to the top of the blade. I didn't know it was that rotten. I whacked it some more and felt a little better. I was about to bring the hoe down again when a thick slab of snake with brown bands and black bands and a triangle head twisted out of the top, darting his tongue at me and coiling up to strike.

I screamed louder than I'd ever screamed in my life, scooped up that snake with the hoe, and slung it into the creek. It slithered over the water to the opposite bank and lay there, coiled up and still. I waited for my heart to slow down and tried not to throw up.

Mama stuck her head out the back door and shouted

to me. I shouted back that everything was all right. I didn't want any help. It was up to me this time, and I knew what I had to do. I went to the bridge and walked over to Mr. Pinky's side of the creek.

The closer I got, the more I didn't want to get there. Why did it matter if I killed that snake now? It would make more sense to go on back to the house and let it lie. But I had to take care of this.

I tightened my grip on the hoe and slid down to where it should have been—but wasn't. I searched up and down the bank on both sides till I had to admit it had swum off down the creek.

I dragged my hoe up the yard. That snake had won.

Willie Jane cried sometimes and didn't try to hide it. She said she liked the family Daddy had found for her, that they were a real nice family and would pay her good wages, but that didn't make our leaving any easier. I told her if it was up to me, we wouldn't be.

When Saturday came, I was sitting on my bedroom floor, packing up the last of my models and board games, when Willie Jane came back to my room saying she had a surprise for me.

"Hey, Trip." It was Dee.

"Dee! You came! I . . . felt so bad about . . . I was hoping that . . ." I got tangled up in my words, and Dee and Willie Jane started laughing, and then I laughed too because I was that happy.

"Don't worry about it," he said. He held out his hand for me to shake, and the clamp I had been carrying inside finally let me go. I reached around and hugged him.

"Good to see you, Trip."

"Good to see you, too."

We sat and talked for a while. He wanted to know what had been going on in the last few weeks, but I didn't tell him everything. I didn't want him to feel like he was the reason bad stuff had happened. We talked about how crummy the New York Giants were this year.

"Seven losses," I said.

"I know," he said.

"The Rebels have lost a bunch of games, too. They need you to hurry up and get to college and be their quarterback. Then they'd win some games, all right."

He didn't smile or anything.

"That's not gonna happen," he said.

"Why not?"

"You know why not."

Of course. Ole Miss doesn't have colored quarterbacks—they don't have a colored player on the team. Dumb again.

We couldn't make pancakes because everything in the kitchen was packed into boxes. Mama brought us breakfast from Primos. I asked Dee if he wanted to play Ping-Pong, and he said he hadn't ever tried it, so we did that awhile and it was okay. We stayed inside the whole morning and on into the afternoon and watched TV and played Chinese checkers and more Ping-Pong—but we both knew the whole time what we really wanted to do was go out in the front yard and throw the football.

The only thing was, I had to ask permission first, and I really didn't want to give Mama another reason to worry. She was pretty well worn-down. There hadn't been any more threats, but Daddy still wanted us inside all the time. Plus, we had to keep everything so clean it looked like nobody lived here. The real estate lady had shown our house to a few people, but nobody wanted to buy it yet. Daddy said it looked like we might have two houses for a while.

The girls were gone to Meemaw and Papaw's all day so Mama and Willie Jane could get everything ready for the movers on Monday. Mama was sitting on the floor in Ginny Lynn's room, boxing up dolls and games. I took a deep breath and stuck my head in the door and tried to make it sound like no big deal:

"Hey, did you know Dee came over?"

"How's ol' Dee doin'?" She had a drop of sweat running down her cheek and was barely listening to me.

"He's fine. We're gonna go out and throw the football a little bit, okay?"

She stopped what she was doing. She was listening now.

"The ground's still wet."

"We don't mind."

"Looks like it might rain some more."

"That's okay."

She sat back on her heels and wiped her face with the back of her hand.

"Well, what the heck. I really do not care what the neighbors think at this point."

"Thanks, Mama."

"Your daddy's pulling his last shift at the hospital and he might have something to say about it when he gets back, so y'all don't—"

"Yes, ma'am." I was already halfway out the door.

We stood at either end of the yard and threw for a while. Then I started running some routes where I would charge off the line of scrimmage and cut in real hard. Dee hit me in the breadbasket every time. I ran some routes all the way down to the other end of the yard, and every time I looked up, the ball would float right into my hands. The unstoppable combo was back in action.

I caught one on the driveway and turned around and yelled "Touchdown!" and there were Stokes and Andy.

"Hey, Trip," Stokes said.

Dee walked over.

I hadn't seen Stokes in a while. He kept looking at

me and then down at the driveway. Him and Andy both looked like they were trying to say something.

"I guess you know we're moving tomorrow," I told them.

"We know," Stokes said. "Listen, you remember that time you and your dad came over and asked if we knew anything about your mailbox getting blown up?"

"Yeah?"

"Well, I did know something."

"What'd you know?"

"I knew that me and Andy blew it up."

"You—you what?"

He looked down at the driveway. "I've been meaning to tell you since I heard y'all were moving." Then he looked back at me. "We didn't do it to make you move away. Everybody kept saying how y'all were so bad for the neighborhood, and . . ."

"We started to believe them," Andy said. "And it was fun to blow something up."

"Yeah," Stokes said. "But we're real sorry. We thought maybe if y'all knew how sorry we were, you wouldn't move."

I opened my mouth but couldn't think what to say. I had to wonder if he was making this up like he made so much other stuff up. But why would he? Then I thought about how I might never see him or Andy again after today.

"You . . . you scared my whole family."

They looked at each other and Stokes finally said, "We're real sorry."

"Well . . . y'all wanna get up a game?"

Andy said we needed more people, and they called Calvin and Kenny. We tossed the ball around, and I told Stokes about the snake, and he said everybody knows cottonmouths like to hibernate in pine stumps. I wished I had known it.

Pretty soon Kenny showed up, then Calvin. He said he told his mom he was just coming over here to say good-bye. I said we better get started because there was no telling how long we had to play before the grown-ups called it off.

It was me, Dee, and Kenny versus Calvin, Stokes, and Andy, just like the first time. I said our team was the Rebels, like always, and Calvin said their team was the Stampede. Andy flipped his buffalo nickel and I called tails. Tails it was.

Dee stripped down to his new T-shirt with no holes and took off his shoes. Calvin set the ball on his tee and backed up to the rose bed to get a good running start. Andy and Stokes lined up with the ball. Calvin made his angry bear face and accidentally cut a big one while he was running up to kick the ball. After that, we called them the Farting Stampede.

It was the same offensive shoot-out we had before. Dee was hitting me for touchdown after touchdown, but Stokes kept his team in the game. He would either complete it to Andy or dump it off to Calvin or keep it himself for a first down and they scored just as much.

Daddy pulled up in the driveway and got out of his car. I ran over to try to explain, but he waved me back and said he was too tired to worry about anything and needed a nap. I told everybody we had to keep the noise down.

After a while there was a sprinkle, and Willie Jane came out and asked us if we didn't have enough sense to come inside. We told her the rain made it more fun. I saw her keeping an eye on us through the living room window.

Other people were watching, too. Word must have gotten around. Mrs. Sitwell watched from her front window. Mr. Nelson watched from his open garage. Cars came by slow, just like before. Then the beat-up white truck drove by with Tim and Tom. I thought at first they were stopping, but they just slowed and then drove on.

"Did you see that?" Dee said. "Those guys."

"I saw 'em," I said. "The police have been to their house, and my daddy has been to their house, and he said if they tried anything, he would shoot 'em. They're not gonna mess with us."

It was Rebels 28, Farting Stampede 28, and we had third down deep in our own territory.

Dee stood behind Kenny to take the snap. I lined up on the far right. Andy was covering me.

"Hut one! Hut two! Hut three!"

Dee backed up with the ball and pumped his arm toward me. I kept running. When I looked back, he had passed it to Kenny and Kenny was trying to pitch it back to him, but Calvin knocked the ball down. Dee scooped it up quick. Andy lost his footing on the wet grass, I cut hard across the middle, and Dee threw it right into my hands.

Stokes dove for me and missed. I carried it into the end zone, threw it in the air, and yelled, "Woo-hoo, mercy! Rebels wi—"

"Hey, jigaboo!"

Tim and Tom came around the Nelsons' hedge. Tom had his bat and there were more guys behind him. I couldn't believe this was happening again on my next-to-last day in the neighborhood.

I wanted to get inside quick—but something stopped me. This was my yard as long as I was standing in it. I had let Dee down before, more than once, but I would not let him down again. I would not spend the whole ride to Kansas City remembering how I had chickened out.

I turned around and took a few steps toward them. "Hi, Tim. Hi, Tom."

"Did y'all want to play?" asked Stokes. "We could pick new sides."

"What's your name, boy?" asked Tim, pointing to Dee.

"His name is—" started Stokes.

"My name is Demetrius Washington," Dee said. Loud.

"Demetrius!" They looked at each other and hooted.

"He goes by Dee," I said, and wished I hadn't, because it sounded like I was apologizing for his name.

They all laughed. "I want to know what the hell he's doing here," said Tom. "I told you what would happen if I saw him in this neighborhood again."

"Dee can play!" I said.

"He ain't gonna play," Tom said.

"He can play better than you!" I yelled.

My hand curled up in a fist without me telling it to. I didn't care if there were more of them than us or if they were bigger than us. I didn't care if it was all-out yard war.

Stokes pulled me by the shoulder and looked at Tom with his eyes wide as they would go, like he needed to tell him something real important:

"Look, y'all, I'll grant you, it looks a little . . . different, this colored kid playing football with us, but he's the maid's boy, see, and we're letting him play with us because . . . because Trip's dad is in there trying to take a nap, and he said he wanted everybody out of the house. He hates any kind of noise when he's trying to sleep. He can't stand it. If y'all keep on making all this racket, you're gonna wake him up and have the wrath of a hundred demons comin' down on you."

"What are you talking about?" Tim curled up his lip.

"Listen, I've seen it," Stokes said. "Me and Clifford Sims were spending the night with Trip, and Clifford got up in the middle of the night to go to the bathroom, and when he flushed the commode, it woke up Dr. Westbrook and he was so mad, he jumped out of bed and went after Clifford and threw him over a coffee table and broke his head open in three places. They had to take the poor guy to the emergency room."

"That's a bunch of bull," Tom said. "Clifford Sims doesn't even live here anymore."

"Why do you think he moved?"

Stokes could tell a great story, but I couldn't let him tell this one.

"No! It's not true what he's sayin'!" I said. "Dee's playing football with us because we want him to. And you don't have to worry about my daddy." I looked him hard in the eye. "You have to worry about me."

"What you gon' do about anything, Dipwad Westbrook?" said Tom, and he shoved me so hard I almost fell backward.

Daddy always said never be the one to start a fight, but always be the one to finish it, and for that, he recommended a hard sock in the nose. Well, they had started this fight.

I looked back at Dee and yelled, *"Dee! Run!"*

Then I turned around and landed my fist on Tom Bethune's nose and knocked him howling to the curb.

He had both hands on his nose and there was blood coming out between his fingers. "It's broke, it's broke. . . ."

Tim slammed his fist into my cheek. He was wearing a ring and blood came away on my hand when I felt where he hit me. Next thing I knew, I was on my back getting kicked by three of them. Through all the legs, I saw Stokes and Andy trying to push them away. And Dee was running right into the fight. I managed to turn over and crawl away from the kicks and get back up again. Johnny Adcock was leaning over trying to help Tom, still moaning. Andy slugged one of the older guys, and they got all tangled up on the ground. Everybody was screamin' and hollerin'. Calvin and Kenny were standing in the rose bed, yelling, "Hit 'em! Hit 'em!"

"Get out of the roses!" I yelled.

Tim slugged me again. Stokes tackled him and before Tim could get up, I got down behind him, pinned his arms back, wrapped my legs around his stomach, and got him in a scissors hold. He was screaming his head off and trying to jab his elbows in me. Stokes picked up the baseball bat and swung it in a half circle to keep the rest of them away while I worked my scissors on Tim. He said if I didn't let him go, he was gonna kill me, which only made me squeeze harder because I figured he was gonna kill me no matter what I did.

Finally, he said, "I give! I give!"

"You give?"

"I give!"

"And y'all will get out of here and leave us alone?" I said.

"Yes, yes! Let go of me!"

"Promise?"

"Promise!"

"No crosses count?"

"No crosses count!"

I let him go.

"That's it, boys!" Tim yelled.

They let go of Andy and everybody got real still.

"Put the bat down, Stokes," I said. "It's over."

Everybody stopped fighting and walked over to us to shake hands and have a truce. I pushed myself off the ground, and as soon as I was standing all the way up, Tim clipped me so hard in the face, everything went brown for a second, and I was down again. When I knew what was going on, he was standing over me with the bat in the air, about to let me have it.

I saw a blur of somebody charging into Tim from the

side and knocking the bat out of his hands, somebody in boxer shorts for some reason. It was . . . Daddy.

"What the hell are you trying to do, son?" He roared it out of his whole body and shoved Tim against the tree by the driveway and pinned him there with the bat across his chest. I had never heard Daddy's voice like that.

"What the hell are you trying to do?"

Tim musta thought he was about to be killed.

"We're sorry, we're sorry. . . ." He looked around for help and his eyes landed on Stokes.

"I told you not to wake him up," Stokes said, and shook his head.

"Yes, you *are* sorry!" yelled Daddy. "You are the sorriest bunch of redneck punks I ever laid eyes on!"

"Don't hurt him, Sam!" Mama yelled from the porch, where she and Willie Jane were standing.

"Dee!" Willie Jane waved for Dee to run up on the porch, but he stayed where he was.

Daddy's eyes were red and squinty. The rain had started coming harder, and his hair was plastered down. He was breathing real hard.

We heard tires screeching, and Mr. Bethune jumped out of his truck so fast he almost fell down.

"What's going on here?" he yelled.

"Your son was about to bring that bat down on my boy's head."

"He broke my nose!" yelled Tom, still holding it with both hands.

"They attacked us!" Tim said. "We were just walking down the street and they attacked us!"

"That's a lie," I said. "We were trying to play football and they walked up and started calling Dee names."

"You see what happens? People get hurt!" yelled Mr. Bethune. "Is that what you want?"

Daddy backed away from Tim and let the bat drop.

"No, Pete, it's what *you* want. You and every redneck in this godforsaken state!"

Mr. Bethune squinted at Daddy and slugged him in the stomach.

Daddy bent over and walked back a few steps with both hands on his gut.

"Whoahhh!" somebody yelled, like when something good happens in a football game.

Mama ran down from the porch but Daddy held out his arm for her to stop.

"It's okay," Daddy said, still bent over. "Go back, go back." His voice was almost not there.

She backed up a few steps, folded her arms, and looked at Mr. Bethune like she wanted to scratch his eyes out.

Mr. Bethune was holding up his fists at Daddy and saying, "Come on! Come on!"

Daddy straightened up again and took a big breath.

"This is not the way, Pete."

"Come on, coward!"

Daddy looked like he was deciding what to do. Then he popped Mr. Bethune hard in the jaw. Mr. Bethune staggered back, rubbed his face. Then he charged at Daddy and took another swing. Daddy dodged it. Then they were all the way fighting.

Mr. Nelson ran across the yard to see better. Mr. Cook stood on the other side of the driveway, smoking a cigarette so hard I thought he might eat it. Stokes's mom drove into her carport, got out, and watched with her mouth open.

"Stokes! Get over here!" she yelled.

Mr. Webb and his boys and the Reeves kids from over on Hartfield were running across the street. They must have heard the shouting. Dr. Reeves was hustling behind them, yelling, "Sock him a good one, Sam!"

I was about to jump on Mr. Bethune's back when Tim went for the bat. I snatched it up before he got there and hurled it into the street. It clanked and rolled, thunder boomed, and the rain came in buckets, like a bat in the street was the signal it had been waiting for. When I turned around, Tim hit me in the stomach the way his dad had hit my dad. Stokes pushed Tim down, and when I looked up again, people were running every which way, and everybody was swinging at everybody. The whole yard was a tangle of arms and legs flying.

Tim and a couple of his buddies were ganging up

on Stokes. Andy was swinging at Johnny Adcock. Mr. Cook tried to stop it and got knocked down. Mr. Nelson tried to help Mr. Cook and got punched, and he started swinging at whoever he could reach. I don't know who Calvin was swinging at. At least he had come out of the rose bed.

I ran over to help Stokes, and Tim spun me around and bloodied the other side of my face. I stood there a second, not feeling anything at all. Then, I felt the monster take over.

"Aaaaahhh!" I landed a sledgehammer fist on Tim's face.

His mouth fell open and he backed away with his hands up. I took a couple of steps toward him. I could have punched out a telephone pole.

That was when the police came.

They hadn't turned on their siren, so everybody was surprised. Those who could scattered. Stokes plopped down on the grass and said he was too tired to run. I plopped by him, panting like a dog. My mouth tasted like blood and dirt and somebody had come along when I wasn't looking and vacuumed every bit of spit out of it. I didn't know what was rain and what was blood, I just knew my face hurt. And my hands hurt. And my legs hurt. And I had never felt so good in my life.

Two policemen got out, one fat, one medium fat, shouting, "Hold it! Freeze right there!"

Let 'em try to take me to jail, I thought. But it wasn't me they were interested in.

It looked like Daddy and Mr. Bethune had gone from fighting each other to hugging. Then I figured out that Mr. Bethune was hanging on to Daddy the way boxers do when they're tired. The policemen told them to freeze again. Anybody could see Daddy and Mr. Bethune were too tired to go anywhere.

Willie Jane was running to the far corner of the yard. "Dee!" she screamed.

I ran over to Dee. He was lying facedown.

"What happened? What happened?" she asked me. I didn't know. I had lost track of him in all the fighting. We turned him over and he had cuts on his face and blood coming from a bad gash. His eyes were open, but I wasn't sure he knew what he was looking at.

"Who got ya? Who did this?"

"Don't know," he mumbled, and grabbed his arm and groaned. "My arm."

I yelled to the policemen to let my daddy come see about Dee, but they were putting handcuffs on him. We got Dee up and helped him inside and laid him down on my bed. Willie Jane held his head and talked to him, and he mumbled something back.

I ran back to see about Daddy, and Mama shoved a shirt and a pair of pants and some loafers at me. "Take these to your father." She didn't want to give them to him herself. It was a good thing those policemen were there, or Daddy would have had another fight on his hands.

"Officer, at least let him get dressed!" Mama yelled from the porch.

Daddy's face was bloody and marked up, and he was breathing hard. I told the policeman I could explain what happened, but he said Daddy and Mr. Bethune could explain it all downtown. I was hoping they'd let Daddy explain why he was in his underwear.

Mr. Bethune started talking real fast, and then he started cussin', and when they tried to calm him down, he swung his arms around, so they took him on to the car.

The medium-fat policeman took the handcuffs off Daddy, just for a minute, he said. "It's against regulations, but under the circumstances . . ."

"I'll be okay, pal," Daddy said to me, stepping into the pants. "Everything will be okay, Virginia!" he yelled to the porch. "Don't you worry! I delivered this man's baby boy, isn't that right, Officer?"

The policeman smiled and nodded.

The other one came back and said to me, "Get on out of the rain, son."

Then they re-handcuffed him and pulled him toward their car.

"It's my fault, Daddy." I had to go ahead and cry, seeing my daddy like that. "All this is because of me."

"Don't you feel bad about a thing, pal," Daddy said over his shoulder. "The good guys won here today."

I didn't know what he meant at first. I had won against Tim, but Daddy and Mr. Bethune had just worn each other down. The bad guys probably threw as many punches as the good guys. I think he meant that the good guys won because we had fought at all. That winning was in not giving in, in trying, no matter how many times you had to try.

Willie Jane put mercurochrome and Band-Aids on Dee's face, and Mama fixed ice packs and a sling made of old sheets for his arm. She told Willie Jane they needed to stay with us, and maybe spend the night, depending on when Daddy got let out of jail. He could say whether the arm was broken or not. Mama thought it was just a sprain.

She looked at my cuts and bruises and declared that I would live. "But you are the wettest little boy I ever saw in my life. Go get cleaned up and I'll put some Band-Aids on you and make you a grilled cheese. Chop-chop!"

I looked in the bathroom mirror at the blood and sweat and dirt all over my face and shirt. I had it all in my mouth, too, and let the shower rinse it out.

Mama fed and doctored me. Willie Jane stayed back in my room with Dee and said she didn't want a grilled cheese, she just wanted her baby boy to be okay. I went into Mama and Daddy's room and lay down on their big bed to rest up a little. My daddy was in jail, and I felt lucky and proud.

When I woke up it was dark. The clock on the nightstand said 8:11. How could that be true? I felt all blurry and sore, and my face had these things on it and it took me a second to remember they were Band-Aids. Willie Jane and Dee were asleep on my bed.

Meemaw and Mama were standing in the middle of the den, hugging. They said hi when I walked through, and kept hugging. I said hi and walked to the kitchen because I was starving.

I fixed a peanut butter and jelly sandwich and stood in the doorway eating it. At first I wanted to hear what they were saying, but after they started talking louder, I wanted them to see me. They wouldn't look over to where I was, only at each other.

"When did he say you could come get him?" Meemaw asked.

"Tonight sometime. One of the officers is being real helpful because Sam delivered his baby last month. Sam will call me." Mama was trying to make her voice sound like Daddy was off on a hunting trip or something. "And Sam is in the right. They came into our yard. Pete Bethune attacked him. Sam said Pete was being so obnoxious they might never let him out." She tried to laugh but it turned into crying.

"Oh, Ginny."

Meemaw hugged her again and took a step back and put her hands on her hips and said, "You know your daddy and I always had our doubts about him."

"Mama, don't."

"Dr. Nobody from Nowhere."

"Please."

"But you were hell-bent for leather to marry him and—"

"Yes, Sam grew up poor, but he worked hard and got scholarships all the way through medical school, and instead of being proud of him for that, you blame him for his childhood."

"After what he said last time y'all had Sunday dinner with us, which was *weeks* ago, I thought, When did my son-in-law become this integrationist? How can he be so wrong in his thinking? But then I said, 'You know, I'm really not at all surprised.'"

"Why is he 'wrong in his thinking' just because he thinks differently from you? Do we all have to be in lockstep about everything?"

"About some things, yes, we do. Unless you want the entire state to go to hell in a handbasket!"

Mama moved away from her. I backed into the kitchen, but not so far I couldn't see.

"And now he's brawling in the yard in front of the whole neighborhood!" She almost shouted it.

"He was *defend*ing himself against the neighborhood. Against people who threatened your grandchildren."

"Hauled off to jail in front of his wife and son! Your husband, a jailbird! The utter disgrace of it!"

"I will not listen to this!"

They stood there and didn't talk for a minute.

Then Meemaw said, "Nobody will tell me to my face, but I know a lot of women have changed doctors."

"And now we're leaving town, so I hope they'll all be very happy."

"Are you really going to take my grandchildren away to a strange Yankee city?"

"Oh, Mama."

She started to cry again, and Meemaw reached out and grabbed her hand.

"Oh, honey, I'm so sorry. It's gonna be okay. It's all gonna be okay." She hugged Mama a little bit and patted her back and smiled the beautiful Meemaw smile and said, "Don't you think it would be better if you let Sam go up to Kansas City by himself for a while and get the lay of the land? You can tell your real estate agent you've decided to put everything on hold for a while. We'll help with the children. We'll give you anything you need. I know it would be hard at first, but it would be for the best." I could hear her smile. "Who knows, Sam might make everybody as mad at him up there as they are down here, and then y'all would just have to move again."

Mama pulled away from her.

"Sam is my husband and where he goes, I go. And I won't hear another word against him, do you hear me? Not another word!"

When Mama settles her eyes on me like that, it means I am in danger, and she was doing it to Meemaw. Except how could that be Meemaw? That lady had just told my mama we ought not to be a family anymore—I didn't know that lady.

I backed all the way into the kitchen and leaned against the counter, where I couldn't see them.

"Well, I better get back to your father," the lady said. "I'm sure he needs my help with the girls. I suppose you'll need us to keep them all night?" She said it like my sisters spending the night at her house would be a lot of trouble. My sisters and I had spent the night with her and Papaw a hundred times!

She rattled around in her purse and her voice came closer.

"I hope it's all right if I get a glass of water before I go," she said.

I backed up more. She stood at the sink and didn't see me. I meant to let her get her glass of water and leave. But I was too mad.

"You can't talk about my daddy like that!"

She spun around.

"Why, Trip! Where did you come from?"

"Daddy . . . he . . . he ran outside and fought to protect me and Dee and my friends. . . . He was fighting for us. . . . He's brave and strong and . . ."

"Your daddy got arrested, honey."

"For doin' the right thing! He works all day and night, doin' the right thing. People come up to me in the grocery store and tell me how he saved their life!" My hands were shaking and my voice was shaking. "You can't talk about him like that! Take back what you said! Take it back!" I wiped my eyes with the backs of both hands. "If you don't take it back, you'll make me . . . I won't forgive you for it," I told Meemaw. "Not ever!"

Mama was standing in the doorway.

"Virginia, you need to see to Trip. He's been very upset by all this. As have we all." She fanned her face with her hand and shook her head. "I don't think the poor boy knows what he's saying. Did he get a concussion?"

Mama looked at her hard and cold. "Trip knows what he's saying."

"We'll meet y'all at church tomorrow with the girls," Meemaw said. She sighed and looked over her shoulder at Mama on her way out. "You know I just want what's best for my baby girl."

"No, Mama. You just want to be right."

. . .

We sat on the couch together. I put my hand on her hand, and she put her arm around me.

I told Mama that now I was glad we were moving, which started me crying more. She stared out the sliding glass door like she was looking at something in the dark.

Willie Jane came into the room.

"You get a good rest, Willie Jane?"

"Yes, ma'am. Dee's still asleep."

"We'll get Dr. Westbrook to check him over when he gets here. I'm sure he'll be just fine."

"He will, he will."

"I hate to ask you to stay, but until I can get back with Dr. Westbrook, I don't have any choice." Mama's eyes squeezed up like she still had more crying to do, and she put her hands to her face, trying not to.

"I can stay."

"Oh, Willie Jane, I just feel so alone in all this."

"You're not alone, Miz Westbrook."

Dee came in after a while, wearing his sheet sling, blinking hard at the lamp. Willie Jane jumped up and hugged him.

"You boys had yourselves quite an afternoon," Mama said.

"Good thing they so tough," Willie Jane said.

"My arm hurts," Dee said.

"Oh, it's not that bad. I'll get you an aspirin and an ice pack."

"I need some Marguerites, too," he said.

"And me," I said.

So Willie Jane made Marguerites, and we ate and talked and waited. At one o'clock, nobody had called from the police station and Mama said it was time for me and Dee to get to bed even if we had had such long naps. She gave Dee my bed, and she tried to give Willie Jane Farish's bed, but Willie Jane said she was gonna stay up as long as Mama did. I got Ginny Lynn's bed, which is barely long enough for Ginny Lynn, and would have done better on the cold, hard floor, but I couldn't sleep much anyway. I kept seeing Mama and that person I didn't know anymore fighting in the den. I watched it again and again in my head, like if I watched it enough times, something would change somehow, and it wouldn't seem so scary and impossible. But the looks and the voices and the words stayed the same until I finally couldn't watch anymore.

Mama and Daddy were eating scrambled eggs and grits and sausages and biscuits at the big table. They said to go into the kitchen and let Willie Jane fix me a plate. Dee was in there, going to town on a biscuit. I was glad they were still here, but I didn't get it.

"Did you sleep okay?" I asked Willie Jane.

"Haven't been to sleep. You?"

"A little. This *is* Sunday, right?"

"That's what I hear."

"You're awful happy for somebody who didn't sleep."

"It's a beautiful day." She pointed out the window. I had to admit the sky was a bright, clear blue.

I sat down at the dining room table and piled up all the scrambled eggs that would stay on a fork and tumped them into my mouth. Then I split a biscuit, put a sausage between the halves, and shoved in as much as would fit.

"Take it easy, greasy, you got a long way to slide." Daddy looked dog-tired, but he was acting all peppy.

"Are you okay, Daddy?" I said.

"Your daddy's feeling pretty chipper, considering what he's been through in the past twenty-four hours," Mama said.

Daddy munched his sausage and nodded and smiled. His eyes had a new kind of light in them. Mama could call it "chipper," but he looked kind of crazy to me.

I took a big gulp of juice and asked the question most kids never get to ask their dads: "So, how was jail?"

"Oh, a very accommodating establishment, jail. The bed's a mite hard and the menu's a bit skimpy, but otherwise most accommodating. Glad to get home to this big country breakfast. How's your face?"

He had Band-Aids on his face too, and his hands and his arms.

"Fine," I said. "How's your everything?"

"Doing well, doing well. Every man needs an old-fashioned fistfight and a night in the hoosegow now and then. Makes you see things in a whole new light."

I wondered if he had been drinking liquor, he was so chipper.

"When you're finished with your breakfast, you need to hurry and get ready for church. It's already too late to make it to Sunday School."

"Do we have to go to church today, after all that's happened?"

"Especially after all that's happened. And look in your closet for some Sunday clothes for Dee," Mama said.

"What?"

"Your mother and I decided it would be good for us all to go to church together," Daddy said.

"Willie Jane and Dee are going to *our* church?"

"I told Willie Jane we would be honored if she and Dee would go to church with us this morning," Mama said.

"And she *wanted* to?"

"She said she did." Either Mama was slap-happy from no sleep, or she had been drinking liquor, too.

"You know what Dee said?" Daddy was beaming. "He said he didn't see how anybody could get mad at a colored boy in God's house. And that's the truth, isn't it? I told your mama, 'Let's do it. Let's really put 'em to the test.'"

I put my hand on his shoulder and said, "Daddy, you don't need to go to church, you need to go to bed."

"Your old dad's used to not sleepin' much, pal."

So I took Dee back to my closet. I found a white shirt and some pants that were okay if he rolled them up. Daddy had made Dee a better sling and told him he didn't think anything was broken, but we would get his arm X-rayed on Monday. Dee said it hurt to move it through the sleeve. I tied his tie for him. My navy blazer didn't swallow him up too bad. He had to roll the shirt cuffs back and pull them together under the coat sleeve.

Mama gave Willie Jane a dark-blue dress that worked pretty well.

Then we all got in the station wagon.

Willie Jane was still so happy. She winked at me like she knew something I didn't.

"And we're off like a herd of turtles," Daddy said.

When you walk through the church door, Mr. Ganderson always smiles like he's saying, "The bigger the smile, the better the Lord likes it," and hands you a bulletin like he's been waiting all week to give you this. But when he saw us this time, his smile shrank up, and he looked at the other ushers like somebody better do something quick.

"They're with me," Daddy said, and we kept walking. Nobody tried to stop us.

Some people looked at us real quick and then looked away, and some kept staring when we turned onto our usual row halfway down on the right, Daddy first, then Mama, then Willie Jane, Dee, and me on the end. Meemaw and Papaw were already sitting with Farish and Ginny Lynn in their usual seats on the opposite side. Papaw had an expression like aliens had landed. Meemaw's lips were pressed hard together and even from across the sanctuary, I could see that her eyes had gone black just like Mama's do. Farish and Ginny Lynn were giggling. Mama flapped her hand for them to sit up straight and hush.

There's usually a lot of talk before the service gets started, but things got real quiet all at once. It was like Dr. Mercer had stuck his head in and shushed everybody. All you could hear was whispering hisses. The choir looked paralyzed. And every one of them was staring right at us.

Sweet old Mrs. Meriweather tapped Willie Jane on the shoulder and smiled real big and said, "Are y'all from the Ethiopian mission?"

"No, ma'am," Willie Jane said. "We're from Jackson."

Mrs. Meriweather looked confused.

Johnny Adcock sat a few rows down with some older guys. I didn't see any Bethunes, so that was good. I hoped they were too beat up to get out of bed.

I asked Willie Jane if she was okay. She nodded, sitting straight as a board and holding on to a little smile. Dee was looking around at everything.

"Is it like your church?" I whispered to him.

"Pretty much. It's a lot bigger. The organ pipes are a whole lot bigger. And we don't have all that up in the back like y'all do, and we don't have a balcony, and we don't have these colored windows with the Bible people on 'em. But it's pretty much the same."

It seemed like it was taking this service an awful long time to crank up. There was nothing to do but listen to the organ, which I personally do not like one bit. Organ music sounds like rotten flowers to me. I heard the ushers talking and kept expecting one to tap me on the shoulder, smile like somebody had died, and ask us to leave.

I leaned over to Mama: "Why hasn't it started?"

"I don't know."

"You think they're waiting for us to get kicked out?"

"Hush."

I could tell she was wondering the same thing.

You're not supposed to rubberneck in church, but I finally had to look behind me. There were the ushers, standing together at the top of our aisle, whispering about what to do with us. It was a relief when the choir director walked out, followed by Dr. Mercer. I didn't know whether he would ask the congregation to welcome us or help the ushers throw us out, but I thought he would say something. It's not like a colored person had ever sat in one of those pews before.

But he held up the palms of both hands, and the ushers went to the back.

Then the choir director told everybody to turn to "Onward, Christian Soldiers" in their hymnals, and we started singing. Everything went on as usual: the welcome, another hymn, a reading from the Bible, another hymn, announcements, another hymn, stand up, sit down.

Then, while the ushers were coming up the aisles with offertory plates, Mr. Goodrich popped up from his seat down front and turned around: "Are we really going to ignore this?" He pointed at Willie Jane and Dee. "Who wants these people in our church? The one place, the *one* place that's still ours? Who wants these people here?"

The organist stopped. Mr. Goodrich yanked his wife up by the hand and she yanked up their boys, and they all marched like good Christian soldiers up the aisle and out the back door.

Then the Thompsons got up and walked out. Then Mr. Newsome. Everybody started talking, not even pretending to whisper. I only heard pieces: "lost their minds"; "insult to the congregation"; "never in all my born days." More walked out.

Mama kept looking across the sanctuary at where

Meemaw and Papaw were sitting with the girls. Meemaw was shaking her head, like "I told you so."

Dr. Mercer was holding out his arms: "Everyone! Please! Please!"

"Tell *them* to leave," yelled Mr. Ganderson from the back. "*They're* the ones should be leavin', not us!"

"Yeah!"

"That's right!"

"Tell 'em, preacher!"

Dee was about to jump up and run, and I was ready to run with him. Willie Jane told Daddy we ought to leave. She was pretty upset.

"We're stayin'," Daddy said in a mean tone of voice. Then he made his voice softer and said, "I think it's important that we stay. If y'all are willing to. They'll settle down."

"Everyone, please calm down!" Dr. Mercer kept saying.

Finally people got quiet. There were half as many there as when the service started. They looked at Dr. Mercer like they were expecting him to say the words that would fix this. I thought he would yell at them for their bad behavior. I was ready for every word of this sermon.

Dr. Mercer folded his hands on the pulpit and looked from one side of the congregation to the other and said, "Perhaps it's best to begin today's message.

I'd like to ask everybody a question today, and I want you to search your hearts before you answer. . . ."

I was thinking he'd say, "Do you believe God only loves white people?" That would be a good question.

". . . And the question is, am I a Mary or am I a Martha? I'll say it again. Am I a Mary or am I a Martha? Turn with me in your Bibles, if you will, to the Book of . . ."

I couldn't believe it. A regular old sermon. Like nothing had happened. In the next thirty minutes, he never said a word about Dee and Willie Jane being there.

We sang "Just as I Am" at the end, which is when people are supposed to come down and ask to be baptized or rededicate their lives and stuff like that. Dr. Mercer waits for them down front and sometimes he talks on the microphone between verses: "Won't you give your heart to the Lord today? Won't you come?" Some Sundays he won't give up until we've sung the hymn through twice. Today we sang two verses and quit. The service was over.

Daddy said to get up and walk out slowly, not like somebody was chasing us. We met Farish and Ginny Lynn in the vestibule and you would have thought they had been away for months, the way they ran up and hugged Mama and Daddy. Daddy said they had to hold all questions until we got to the car.

Dr. Mercer was standing at the top of the tall steps,

shaking everybody's hands as they came out, like he always does. Papaw was having a long talk with him. Daddy guided us around them, and we started down.

"Go back to your own kind," came a kid's voice behind us.

"And stay gone!" yelled Johnny Adcock.

Him and his friends yelled more ugly stuff. I heard adult voices, too.

"You must stop this immediately!" Dr. Mercer said.

They didn't stop.

"Keep walking," Daddy said. "Don't look at them."

I had to turn once, real quick. Dr. Mercer was holding his arms out, looking back and forth at everybody. Some of them were waving their fists. Papaw was just standing there looking confused in a way I've never seen Papaw look. When I looked back around, Meemaw was halfway down the steps with us, putting her arm around Mama.

"Honey, oh, honey, I don't understand what you're doin', but . . . I'm still your mama," she said. "I'm so sorry . . . about . . . about . . ." And she started crying. Then Mama started crying. We stood at the bottom of the steps while they hugged and cried, while people streamed by us or yelled down at us.

The sun was so bright I could hardly open my eyes against it to see where the station wagon was parked. Meemaw hugged Mama one last time and went back to find Papaw.

"Okay, we're to the car," said Farish. "You said you would tell us."

"Daddy got in a fight, sweetheart. But it's all gonna be okay."

We were all standing at the back of the station wagon.

"The church is mad at us," Ginny Lynn said.

"Maybe it's not our church anymore," Daddy said.

"Who were you fighting, Daddy?" Farish asked.

"We were fighting lots of people," I told her. "They got me on both sides of my face. The police came and everything."

"Police?"

Daddy looked up at the sky, and I knew I shouldn't have said that.

"Did you have to go to jail?" Farish asked.

Mama shook her head at me and Daddy, like "Don't talk about it."

But Daddy said, "Just for a little while."

"Did Trip have to go to jail?" asked Ginny Lynn.

"No, darlin'."

"But they let you out?" asked Farish.

"Oh, yeah. They let me off with a slap on the wrist."

Farish looked at Mama with her eyes wide. "They *slapped* him? I didn't think policemen were supposed to *slap* people."

"It's an expression, Farish. Y'all get on in the car."

"Hold it, everybody," Daddy said, looking at Mama like he was asking her permission.

"Tell 'em right here?" Mama asked.

"It's the perfect time and place."

"Go ahead."

Mama was smiling, so it didn't make sense when Daddy said, "Children, I'm afraid we've got some bad news for you."

Farish held her breath like we were driving through a tunnel.

"You know those packed-up boxes all over the house?"

We knew, we knew.

"We don't have to put them in the moving van ourselves, do we?" Farish said.

"Nope." He smiled big. "You have to help your mama and me unpack 'em."

"Unpack 'em?" the girls said together.

"You mean . . . ?" I was afraid to believe this could be true.

"We're not moving after all," Mama said, and sighed. "We're stayin' right here in Jackson."

"Yippee!" The girls screamed and jumped and held hands and danced in circles, singing "We're not moving, we're not moving. . . ."

This was such unbelievable news, so not what I expected, I was numb for a second. Then I couldn't stop hugging them. "Oh man, oh man! When— How did this . . . ?"

Then I was hugging Willie Jane and saying, "This is why you were so happy! You knew!"

"I didn't know for sure, I just prayed it was so. I had a feeling the way your daddy was talkin' this morning when he came back from the jailhouse, he looked at Miz Westbrook and he said, 'So are we gonna move or are we gonna stay and fix this?' He said all the Bethunes in this world couldn't run him away, that he had almost let it happen. He said he wasn't gonna run from anybody. Your daddy's a strong man, Trip. A strong man."

Everybody was hugging and laughing.

"But what about the people saying they're gonna hurt us?" Farish was out of breath from all her dancing and singing.

"They're trying to scare us, sweetie," Daddy said. "But that doesn't mean we have to be scared."

"Careful," Mama said. "But not scared."

Daddy said we should celebrate with some ice cream, so we drove to the Seale-Lily and ordered six banana splits to go. Mama and Ginny Lynn shared theirs. Dee cradled his in his sling, and we raced to see who could finish his first. Farish raced with us, even though Mama told her she couldn't. I got a headache from trying to eat it too fast and had to let Dee win.

When Willie Jane and Dee had changed back into their clothes, we hugged them good-bye.

"See you tomorrow!" It felt so good to say it.

That night, Daddy came into my room before I went to sleep. He said he had a long time to sit and think in that jail cell, a longer time to sit and think than he'd had in years, and two lightbulbs came on in his head while he was there.

The first lightbulb told him that no matter what had happened, Mama didn't really want to leave her hometown. Things would be different here now, but Jackson was where she had lived her whole life except for when she went to Sophie Newcomb, and no matter how hard he tried to make her happy in Kansas City, he knew she'd be miserable there or anywhere besides her hometown.

"There's home and there's everywhere else," he said. "Jackson is home, like it or not."

He let me think about that a minute.

"Anyway, we'd be letting everybody down if we moved, right?" he said.

"You mean Willie Jane and Dee?"

"Yep. The whole state, too. We all have a responsibility to each other."

"Just because we live in the same place?"

"It's a special kind of place, don't you think?"

"A special kind of terrible sometimes."

"Sometimes it is. But there are a lot of good people here, pal, who want the best for everybody. They're the ones who aren't shouting and shaking their fists. Only half the congregation walked out, right?" He smiled. "The half that stayed, that's the future."

"Maybe so, but the rest of the world still hates us."

"Hey, the world needs to understand that it wouldn't be the same without Mississippi. Think about the books and the music that have come from here. Without us, you wouldn't have the blues, which means you wouldn't have rock 'n' roll, which means no Elvis, no Beatles. And what about the food? You can't get Willie Jane's fried chicken and mashed potatoes just anywhere, you know."

"You sure can't."

"I tell ya, Trip, it's like one day God took the best of what's good and the worst of what's bad, stirred it all up, and dumped it between Memphis and New Orleans. You can't move away from a place like that. You have to help keep the good in the mix."

He patted me on the shoulder and stood up.

"What about the other lightbulb?" I asked. "You said there were two."

"The other lightbulb came on when I was sitting there feeling how bad my body hurt and asking why I had allowed myself to get all beat up and thrown in jail. The first answer was I did it to protect you. But I also did it to defend our right to have anybody we like play football in our own front yard. I told myself that if I really believed in that, I had to be willing to fight for it, maybe not just once, maybe again and again. Moving away would be running away, no matter what we kept telling ourselves. And Westbrooks don't run. Do we?"

"No, sir."

"You helped me remember that, Trip. Watching the way you fought for Dee. You're a hero."

"Hero? I thought I was a goof-up."

He laughed and hugged me.

"I bet all your patients will be glad you're not leaving the clinic."

"I'll tell you something, I'm thinking about starting my own clinic. One that'll have a big waiting room where everybody can sit."

As much as I hated to move away from 5445 Oak Lane Drive, the house I had lived in my whole life, it was not safe to stay there. Stokes and the Reeveses and Mr. and Mrs. Pinky were still our friends, but that was it.

I thought and thought, but I couldn't understand how these neighbors who acted so mean used to be so nice. The closest I could figure, their version of the world was all black and white, and not only in terms of people's skin. They carried a big line in their heads between what was okay and what was not okay, and I had crossed it. So they looked at me with their real faces like I was the one who had changed . . . into somebody bad and stupid and dangerous. They were the same neighbors they had always been—I just never really knew them before.

We finally found out who was making all the calls. It was the Bethunes, like we thought, and their friends, but it was also the Nelsons, the Stubbses, Mrs. Sitwell, and lots of other people. They had gotten together and decided to drive us out of Oakwood. Mr. Bethune held meetings at his house and told everybody we were in league with the Northern agitators and the Freedom Riders, and they needed to send us the message that they didn't want colored kids playing with their kids, and they didn't want coloreds taking over the Southern way of life. Daddy said it showed how pathetic they were, that they thought hang-up calls were a way to fight the federal government. We never found out who threatened me and my sisters.

I can still see Mr. Bethune's angry, puffed-up face and wonder how that could be the same person who always grinned at me in church and called me a wisenheimer. Where did he get so much hate? If he hadn't taught it to Tim and Tom, they might have played with us instead of worrying about what color Dee was.

A lot of things are different now, and mostly better.

Willie Jane is still my other mama—that's not going to change. We moved to a big old house in an older neighborhood closer to town and got a private phone number we don't give out to anybody unless Mama and Daddy know them. Daddy wears one of those new pagers on his belt to keep up with his patients. The phone still rings a lot, mostly with calls from Farish's friends, and I still cringe a little every time.

We don't belong to the country club anymore. Daddy says he can't believe he ever wasted time playing golf. We don't go to Broadview Baptist Church anymore either. Mama and Daddy have been getting together with some people who think like they do, and they're talking about starting up their own church, with a preacher who not only isn't afraid to talk about colored people but would also welcome them into the congregation.

We still live close enough to Donelson Junior High for me to go there, and I am finally a split end for the Donelson Dirt Daubers—third string, so far, but Coach says I have a lot of potential. People still talk about me and my family, but I'm learning not to care what people say. The Bethunes have gone on to high school, so I don't have to fool with them anymore. Stokes and I are back to being best friends. I'd rather have one or two good friends than be popular. Andy's still my pal, and I asked Nancy Harper to go to the homecoming dance. I'm kind of nervous about it, but I figure if we run out of things to talk about, we can always make fun of each other's accents.

Roderick's parents took him out of Donelson right when I was getting to know him. Over the summer, some people blew up his dad's dental clinic one night, just like they said they'd do. Miss Hooper told me his family moved to Tupelo. Nancy and I talk about going up to see him one day.

Mama and Daddy say the schools are about to be completely integrated, along with restaurants, hotels, movie theaters, and everything else. They say it's going to happen fast, and whites will be slow to accept it.

Mama says she's learning not to care what people say, too, and she can't believe it has taken her this long. She doesn't go to Junior League and garden club meetings as much now. She's spending a lot of time tutoring Dee and some kids from his neighborhood who want to go to a better school. She says Dee's a whiz at math.

We don't eat Sunday dinner with Meemaw and Papaw that much anymore, and everybody seems to watch their words when we do. Meemaw never has told me she's sorry for what she said about Daddy. She wants to smile and act like it never happened and seems to expect me to do the same. But every time I look at her, I see that night. Daddy says he's about to convince Papaw to help him fund a new clinic near where Willie Jane lives. It will be for women who can't always go to the doctor because they can't afford it.

Tomorrow is Saturday and Dee will be coming over. I told Willie Jane to be sure and wake me up early so we can make pancakes before the game. Stokes will be here after lunch. Andy finally ran out of excuses and admitted that his mom wouldn't drive him to my house. Guys from the new neighborhood have been showing up, though, and we usually have at least three-man teams. My yard is even better for football now, with hardly any trees.

I have more reasons than ever to live in this place that I love and hate and never will understand. Sometimes, when I think about everything Willie Jane and Dee and me and my family went through last fall, and what everybody in Mississippi will have to go through before things get much better, I feel pretty hopeless. Then I remember what Daddy said after the yard war: "The good guys won here today." They just might win tomorrow.

AFTERWORD

The Jackson, Mississippi, of this novel is based on the one I remember from 1964, though characters, churches, neighborhoods, and schools have been fictionalized. There really was a Willie Jane, I did throw a football with her son in our front yard, and the neighbors did object. That would not happen today.

I have tried to give my characters language true to the time. When I was growing up, the terms *Negro* and *colored* were used by whites who wanted to separate themselves, at least superficially, from those who showed no respect for blacks and commonly tossed around the offensive *nigger*. I have made an effort to keep that word and other epithets to a minimum, using them only as signifiers of the racism this story deplores.

A younger, more creative and generous spirit enlivens the neighborhoods where I grew up. Some things, like passionate football rivalries and surpassingly delicious food, will never change and never should. But Jackson is different in a thousand ways from what it was in 1964, and incalculably better in one way: now it belongs to everybody.

ACKNOWLEDGMENTS

Deepest gratitude to my brilliant, witty, and tireless agent, Molly Ker Hawn of the Bent Agency, who believed in this book and made it happen; to the incomparable Wendy Lamb, who pointed me in all the right directions, to assistant editor Dana Carey and readers Sarah Eckstein, Hannah Weverka, Teria Jennings, Alexandra West, and Alex Borbolla; to my wife, Beth, and my children, Mary Katherine and J.T., for changing the world from black-and-white to color; to Mama and Daddy for more than I can say or repay; to Min, Ken, Mabs, and Banana for love, forbearance, and dessert; to my beloved uncle Barry Hannah, constantly missed, who taught me about writing and laughing and yard ball; and to Willie Jane, wherever she may be.